ATLANTASTAN 2

CHRIS GREEN

URBAN AINT DEAD

URBAN AINT DEAD
P.O Box 448
Maybrook, NY 12543

No part of this book may be reproduced or transmitted in any form by any means, electronic or mechanical, including photocopying, recording, or by any information storage system, without written permission from the publisher.

Copyright © 2024 By Chris Green

All rights reserved. Published by URBAN AINT DEAD Publications.

Cover Design: P. Wise / The Wise Services

Edited By: Shawna Brim / Ladies Of Lit

URBAN AINT DEAD and coinciding logo(s) are registered properties.

No patent liability is assumed with respect to the use of information contained herein. Although every precaution has been taken in the preparation of this book, the publisher and the author assume no responsibility for errors or omissions. Neither is any liability assumed for damages resulting from the use of the information contained herein. This is a work of fiction. Names, characters, places, and incidents are either the product of the author's imagination or are used fictitiously. Any resemblance to actual events, locales, or persons living or dead is entirely coincidental.

Contact Author at FB Author Chris B. Green / IG: @_authorchrisgreen / TikTok: @_authorchrisgreen

Contact Publisher at www.urbanaintdead.com

Email: urbanaintdead@gmail.com

Print ISBN: 979-8-9904701-8-7

STAY UP TO DATE

To stay up to date on new releases, plus get information on contests, sneak peaks and more,
Click the link below...
https://mailchi.mp/6d21003686d1/subscribe

CONTENTS

Soundtracks · 9
Urban Aint Dead · 11
Submissions · 13

1. Rude Boy · 15
2. Shanti · 24
3. Lo · 34
4. Agent Jamiyah Porter · 45
5. Rude Boy · 58
6. Agent Jamiyah Porter · 66
7. Taki · 80
8. Rude Boy · 93
9. Agent Jamiyah Porter · 105
10. Rude Boy · 118
11. Agent Jamiyah Porter · 127
12. Taki · 135
13. Dahlia · 145
14. Taki · 156
15. Agent Jamiyah Porter · 162

Review · 173
Other Books By · 175
Coming Soon From · 179
Books By · 181
Stay Connected · 183

Soundtracks

Scan the QR Code below to listen to the Soundtracks/Singles of some of your favorite U.A.D titles:

Don't have Spotify or Apple Music?
No Sweat!
Visit your choice streaming platform and search URBAN AINT DEAD.

Currently on lock serving a bid?
JPay, iHeartRadio, WHATEVER!
We got you covered.

Simply log into your facility's kiosk or tablet, go to music and search URBAN AINT DEAD.

URBAN AINT DEAD

Like & Follow us on social media:
FB - URBAN AINT DEAD
IG: @urbanaintdead
Tik Tok - @urbanaintdead

Submissions

Submit the first three chapters of your completed manuscript to urbanaintdead@gmail.com, subject line: Your book's title. The manuscript must be in a .doc file and sent as an attachment. The document should be in Times New Roman, double-spaced, and in size 12 font. Also, provide your synopsis and full contact information. If sending multiple submissions, they must each be in a separate email. Have a story but no way to submit it electronically? You can still submit to URBAN AINT DEAD. Send in the first three chapters, written or typed, of your completed manuscript to:

URBAN AINT DEAD
P.O Box 448
Maybrook, NY 12543

DO NOT send original manuscript. Must be a duplicate.
Provide your synopsis and a cover letter containing your full contact information.
Thanks for considering URBAN AINT DEAD.

RUDE BOY

District 7

The last few days had been hell on wheels for me and my team. I was losing so many soldiers, and I still had to make the biggest decision in my life with how I chose to deal with Taki. I was lost for words and emotions when I looked back on how she betrayed me, how she betrayed my team. I would have never seen deceit in her for any reason at all, and no one could have convinced me that one day I would be standing against the same woman that I called a best friend.

"Rude Boy, I'm not sure if it's wise to sit back and wait on this girl to move. You see we're already at an advantage, and the longer we procrastinate, the more opportunity she has to win," Ghost said.

"Understood, but this isn't the average woman we're dealing with here. Taki is intelligent, and she knows everything about me. I have to move correctly because one mistake and it'll be my last."

"I have an idea." Agent Porter stood to her feet.

Since I'd saved her ass a few days back, her mind was grounded on us helping each other. She wanted to see the end of the Kiss Squad, and I wanted the same, just with Shanti added in the deal. There was no other way around that demand, and I was going to do whatever to see it happen.

"What? Because we're only here together for one reason, but don't get the thought in your little brain that you run this show at all. I can't risk Shanti for you, this team, or nobody else." I cut her off immediately.

"If it ain't for the team, why the hell are we here? You damn sure not doing this alone, and I'm surely not killing motherfuckers I'm not even beefing with on the strength of a chick that I'm not smacking," Seven voiced, causing me to look at him.

Before I could think twice, I was in his face within a blink, breathing down his neck like a rabid dog. Nobody made decisions but me when it came to the way I operated my crew, and it wasn't about to start today.

"Fuck the way you feel, nigga! You absolutely right. You not here for my team or my bitch. You damn sure would never even touch a bitch of my girl's caliber, so I can see where your stupid ass statements are coming from. You here on the strength of your uncle and your own beef with Lo. Atlantastan owes me a lot, and obviously, it holds something for you too because you made the decision to be here, nigga. Watch your mouth on how you stepping because the door is open to leave whenever you feel. Your services come with compensation so remember this is business, Seven." I looked him square in the eye.

I watched JoJo clutch on his Glock quietly in the corner as if he was prepared to take out anyone in the living room for me. Shit was jumbled up so much that he didn't know who we should trust or if things would go right dealing with this fucking Fed that was hounding me to help her.

"Hey! Right now is not the fucking time for you guys to be acting like enemies. I'm not standing here for any reason as well and remember that you all are criminals that's supposed to be dead or under the prison for the actions you've made in this state. I'm looking beyond that and viewing you all for what's at stake right now — a concerned family that's willing to do anything to have their relative back. So, I don't wanna be in charge of anything, but you can bet your asses there will be no moves made without me being aware. Now, I can help you all, and in exchange, you'll help me, but you have to listen." Agent Porter cut us off with authority booming in her voice.

I wasn't into debating, neither was I about to lose the opportunity to bring Shanti home to me and her father. Right now, Agent Porter was my only help to seeing any daylight on that, and I needed her help, no matter how shit looked at the moment. I was going to kill everyone involved with this step by step. I just needed to get Shanti back first. For some reason, I just kept having the same feeling in my heart to not trust this cop ass bitch.

"So, what the fuck are you suggesting?"

We all sat back and listened to her plans, and I caught the same distrust for the pig in Ghost's eyes when he glanced over at me. His opinion alone was enough, not only because I knew he was smart but because he moved like me in so many ways. The respect was mutual, and I knew for a fact that him and JoJo would be standing beside me when the smoke cleared.

Once she was done giving her insight, we set up a destination to meet tomorrow after she made her move, and I prayed that it worked in some form of way. I didn't care if she warned me against all altercations until we were in a better position. Someone would die every night until all these situations faded.

"I don't trust that bitch not one bit. I've been around this city and in this game for a long time. Her kind is the type that loves to blind. If I feel she's moving flaky in any way, I'm gonna shoot her ass in the back of the head. I move alone when it comes to surviving, but I'm with you through this mud until you can step out. I'll be in the guest room." Ghost excused himself.

Seven watched him until he exited my living room. He made a remark under his breath before making his way out the front door. I didn't want to have any suspicion on the way he was moving, and I respected Sami so much, but I wouldn't hesitate to get rid of him if necessary.

"What are we gonna do, Rude?" JoJo asked me as I continued to stare at the ceiling.

"We're gonna get Shanti back and kill everyone that we possibly can who violated this team. After this is over, we're giving this shit up and relocating. Expand on another level. I'm leaving this city of havoc behind me." I exhaled, thinking about the rage I was intending on releasing.

"Whatever you say." He nodded before taking a seat quietly back in the corner.

∼

District 4
Agent Jamiyah Porter
Federal Interrogation Building

THE MORNING I LEFT MY HOME, I ALREADY HAD THE MINDSET on making this fucking guy pay for all the torment that he'd committed to this force and city, but of course there was always a superior somewhere in the mix that had an input on what my objective was. I headed out toward District 4, the Zone 3 area where the office for federal interrogation was normally held. My chief was ordering me not to proceed with anything dealing with the Kiss Squad on my own, a direct order that I chose to let go in one ear and out the other.

I pulled into the facility and quickly made my way inside. My Christian Louboutin heels clinked across the marble floors as I paced toward my destination. I sported a white Dior two-piece suit that made me catch a few eyes with every strut. It wasn't my mission to make anyone lust for me, but it was my intention to make a man submit to the will of a woman. In the end, this was all bigger than us. I needed the Kiss Squad out of Atlantastan, and I meant out for good, even if it meant placing a bullet in each of their heads to diminish the crime rate on homicides.

"Good morning, Ms. Porter. The defendant should be here soon," an on-duty guard informed me as he opened the door to the interrogation room.

"Thanks."

I politely took a seat at the table and viewed a few documents in my binder. I was aware of a lot of things I shouldn't know about this guy, and I was going to use all that to my advantage.

After a few minutes of silence, the doors opened, and two guards entered with Tizo shackled and bound in cuffs. He was not only one of the most wanted men in Georgia, but he was the top killer for the Kiss Squad. He was probably responsible for more murders than most of the crews in Atlanta combined. If he declined my offer, not only would he be confined for eternity, but there would never be any awareness if he happened to get a surprise death visit at his cell door after so long.

Sitting him down in front of me, the two officers standing post with me stood firmly at his sides. I closed my binder, looking him in the eyes.

"Do you know who I am?"

"No, and why should I give a fuck, but it's clear that you're related to a fucking pig, punta!"

I could see the anger on his face, and he had yet to understand that I got my way when it came down to protecting and serving under my oath.

Nodding to one of my guards, he grabbed Tizo by the back of the head, ramming his face against the table twice.

"Agghh. What the fuck… what the fuck is this?" His eyes grew wide in pain as his nose started to pour blood profusely.

I grabbed a few napkins from my handbag, tossing them on the table with a smile.

"I'll tell you exactly what it is. It's an offer, Tizo. According to the streets, you're responsible for over forty murders through these Atlanta districts, so I can finally say that I have enough to slam your soul our for twenty generations. I also know that your dad, Hernandez Diablo, has a ten-million-dollar bounty on your head for your betrayal to his cartel in Mexico. Now, how I know this is none of your business, but I also know that you might need my help if you wanna continue to live and make it out of these chains one year within the next sixty," I stated calmly.

Just from the look on his face, I could tell that I had struck a few nerves. The sound of his father's name caused his eyes to widen. It wasn't hard to get info about any criminal in this city, especially when it was mainly run by criminals. I was precise about every step I made, and I never played checkers over chess.

"What the fuck do you want from me?" He looked crazy, gritting his teeth.

"Easy. You're gonna help me bring the Kiss Squad down. It took me a while to see that this operation wasn't just the most dangerous but one of the most diverse organizations in this city. I never knew that Kiss was a woman. All these years, you guys ran orders and murdered from the call of a woman."

"A very dangerous woman," he replied, trying to control his breathing.

"Explain." I crossed my legs and gave him the floor.

"First of all, you're gonna get everyone you love killed. I'm not sure what you have on your agenda, but Taki is not going to bow, bend, or break. She has her own set agenda, and I can promise it's gonna take more than what you got to stop her."

"Her agenda consists of what?" I smirked.

"She wants Rude Boy. You're dealing with a psychopath that has scorned her own soul from being in love, and she is onboard for all the fuckery. I worked beside her for years, and the only thing that disheveled her brain is feigning for a man that she can't have."

"Sounds like a jealous bitch to me. I could care less about her wanting to suck off Rude Boy, neither do I care about her mental health dilemma, because my job is to do one thing. Bring this bitch down. The girl, Shanti, Rude Boy's wife, you're gonna tell me where she is and help me take Taki down. You do that and you can consider yourself a ghost for this federal bureau."

"I'm willing to help under one condition."

"I'm still standing here," I stated with my patience wearing thin.

"Get me out of the country so my father will never find me."

I weighed his request, and at the moment, I had no time to even debate. If I could track down Taki, I could bring the entire Kiss Squad to an end.

"I'll do it under one condition, and you have my word. Give me the location on where she's holding the girl, and you will be taken care of."

"This will not end well, but you have a deal." He held his hand out.

I nodded and walked out of the room, leaving his cuffed hand dangling in the air. I would usually never make alliances with a criminal, but I needed this pandemonium to end.

SHANTI

I was so scared and lost at the moment. It was like my heart knew that Rude would put the word out for someone to come and get me, but as time went on, I started to feel more down about making it out of this place alive. These assholes moved my location to a filthy apartment that had the stench of ten dirty hookers in the air. Part of that stench was coming from me not being able to bathe my own ass, and I was starting to hate everything about my life with each second that passed.

The sound of Polar coming through the front door caught my attention. Even though I was in a bedroom, I could clearly hear the voice of Taki with him.

"Where is she?" Her tone was harsh as I listened to the footsteps grow closer to where I was bound.

The moment both of them stepped in the room, she glared

at me with hatred, and I didn't hesitate to match her nasty gaze.

"You dirty bitch. You have to be so desperate to think you can just do this to me as if it wouldn't be any consequences after the smoke is clear."

She wasted no time backhanding me forcefully, and I could taste the blood that was starting to drip in my mouth. I spit it on the floor next to me and looked directly back up into her face. She smirked evilly before leaning over.

"I can explain this to you for sure. I never liked you, never cared that you even existed if I should say so myself. You've had the golden life of sampling my dick for too long. Rude Boy is just lost in a dilemma right now, and that's perfectly fine. I built the Kiss Squad with my own hands. The status of beefing with the man I've always carried so much love for was beyond my agenda. It's so beautiful how you can plan another's defeat. I knew that you would be my problem one day. So, I plotted ahead. I can offer you this. You can keep your life and disappear, leave Rude Boy for me to handle, and go enjoy your rich life with another cock in Germany somewhere. Atlantastan belongs to me, but I need my king to see that. It's impossible to see that happen with you around, boo boo." She tapped her finger across my nose.

I started to feel my chest flare up with rage. The audacity this bitch had, and just her mentioning how she tricked my man had me wanting to tear this girl's soul out of her body.

"Bitch, make it easy then. Go ahead and kill me so we can

crash and burn it all cause I can guarantee you're not gonna win. Rude Boy didn't trust you as a friend. He trusted you as a worker, you fucking psycho. You were never of any importance, and the feelings have always been mutual, Taki. You're gonna end up with a tombstone directly over your fucking skull." I struggled in the restraints, wanting to put my hands on her so bad.

Polar stood back against the wall on his crutches, and I could see in his face that he was starting to have doubts about the trail they were treading down.

"See, you don't understand. I can't just kill you, no matter how bad I could easily just slit your throat right now. I need Rude Boy to see the deceit in you, the will that you left on your own because you were just not built for this life. I can accept nothing less. I need his pain and manhood to drill inside of me, so you can be a memory. I can't have my husband mad at me for wasting your life. If I can get him to see that I was only doing him a favor by removing you, I can have the dream that I already envisioned with him."

"That'll never happen, Taki. You think you can just betray Rude and there will be no pain behind that, and that's where you're so dumb. You're already dead, you and your punk ass brother standing behind you. Ask him, he knows." I smirked, trying my best not to cry.

Taki spun her head around, looking at his nervous expression.

"What the fuck is that supposed to mean?"

"Taki, she's just trying to get in your head. I don't know what the fuck it means, but I do feel that we need to start making a decision with this shit. Chaos City Day is set for five more days, and we got people dropping by the day. We won't win this war if you're chasing after him instead of the city."

She gritted her teeth at him and snatched the small Beretta handgun from the side of her hip.

"I decide what moves are made and what's not. I built this, and Rude Boy is my piece that's missing!"

She turned, placing the gun in my face, and I knew that she wouldn't hesitate to shoot. The bitch was a lunatic. Even the few times I met her around my man, it was never a positive energy flowing from her skin. I never voiced my opinion back then, and now I was falling from that same mistake.

"I should blow your little brains all over that window behind you. The minute I get Rude Boy to agree with my decision on our marriage, the quicker I can let you be my brother's sex slave. If he refuses, he'll die as well, and then we'll all bleed in harmony," she threatened, pressing the barrel of the gun in my face harder. "I want you to meet up with Daffy and come up with whatever you can. I want that entire district ripped apart, and Rude Boy is the only thing I need to see standing at the end. Now!" She stormed out of the room.

I glanced up at Polar, who looked like he was being pushed off the edge of a cliff. I knew that he didn't want to test Rude because he knew exactly what his fate would be. I just prayed that my husband was able to reach me in time.

Daffy

Ever since I started to build my money and form my own plans without Rude Boy, I was receiving magnificent results. This was the life that any real gangsta would want. Anyone who wanted to be their own boss would take the same steps I had in my shoes as well. This was only the beginning. Since I linked in with the Kiss Squad, I was already pushing weight to the Hispanics out in District 5. My name was ringing bells because I was doing the things another muthafucka wasn't willing to do, not to mention I was always going to stick and move because I knew more about this game than anyone. This city was designed for your death. If you sat still long enough, you wouldn't have to worry about too many days coming after.

Pulling down to the end of our border zone in District 10, I turned inside of the Texaco gas station and parked my car next to Polar's young assassin, Jayo. A few Kiss Squad members moved about, hugging the corners like street signs, and I wasted no time jumping out so I could get this cap ass meet up over and done.

"Yo, where the fuck is Polar?" I asked Jayo before I lit up a Newport.

He motioned with his head to follow him and walked me to the side of the building where a large hot wing stand sat. A few cars were parked, including Polar's, and the small crowd that was gathered around looked as if they had started this shit without me.

"Damn, looks like I'm late or y'all really didn't need me to hear what was going on." I smirked arrogantly.

"Man, we don't got time for all that, Daffy. You know we need you here, and I'm only calling all of us together for one reason — to get this shit over with so we can all sleep peacefully in our own city."

I laughed, pulling out a twenty-dollar bill for a ten-piece wing set up. I was hungry, and Polar was acting as if he was finally ready to put in some real work. This was a conversation I needed a front row seat for.

Paying for my chicken, I sat on the hood of his car as he spoke to the few soldiers that were posted around us.

"Now we all know that Rude Boy has been dropping our team down in these streets since Lo pressed the button for Chaos City Day. We have to end this shit because the boss ain't having no understanding on what's next. She wants the entire District 7 for herself, but she does not want this nigga, Rude Boy, killed. If he dies, all this shit around us falls."

I bit a piece of one of the wings and literally almost tossed that shit to the ground when I heard the stupid ass statement leave his mouth. If we weren't killing Rude, what the fuck were we doing because it clearly wasn't any understanding on that nigga's end when it came down to us? I knew Rude better than anyone standing in the damn parking lot, so agreeing to sign my own death certificate by not blowing this nigga's head off was out of the question.

"What the fuck do you mean don't kill him? Nigga, what the fuck does this look like, *Menace II Society*? This isn't a damn movie, Polar. Do you know what this nigga is capable of? I don't think you do because if you did, you wouldn't be saying that shit. I don't give a fuck what the boss said. I will never be a sitting duck for anyone. You think he playing about that bitch, Shanti? He'll kill every motherfucker out here bout that hoe."

The sound of a car skating out of control caught my ear, and by the time we all looked around, there was an all-black Toyota truck smashing directly through the wing stand, causing dust and glass to fly everywhere. We all slowly scattered, trying to figure out what the fuck just happened, and seconds later, three black Yukon trucks sped into the small parking lot. I didn't hesitate to pull my gun, and as the doors to the truck opened, the first face my eyes landed on was Rude's. He wasted no time killing one of the Kiss Squad members as soon as his feet touched the pavement.

Our crew pulled their guns, but we were a beat short because the eight people this nigga brought along were aiming at us like a target practice. I still held my position with my burner in the air, getting as much distance as I could.

"Long time no see, pussy!" Rude held two Glocks in his hands, pointing them directly at Polar. Even though the Kiss

Squad members didn't bail out on him immediately, he was stuck like a deer on a car bumper.

"You might wanna be easy, Rude. You kill me, you will never get Shanti back. It's rules to this shit, my nigga. The sun is still up, and you're in my district." Polar tried to reason with this nigga on the low.

"Fuck that! Kill him or we're all gonna die. We might as well gun this shit out cause I'm not letting down my guard with this fool!" I shouted with anger.

Rude Boy's eyes found me, but he didn't say a word. His stare was enough, and I knew that he was salty about the betrayal between me and his crew.

"I've been up night and day. Our issues have gotten far beyond the means of talking, and you've crossed the line with implementing my girl in a man's beef. Fuck what you think I shouldn't do," Rude Boy stressed before pulling the trigger to his guns.

Boom! Boom!

The two slugs found their home inside Polar's chest, and I watched him drop to his death. Within seconds, bullets were flying across the parking lot.

Poc! Poc! Poc! Poc! Poc! Poc!

Everybody was shooting, and I didn't wait to break for cover. His team had a set mission and watching a few of the Kiss Squad members get slaughtered ensured me that there would be no win. Rude was too strapped, and I didn't plan on dying today for free.

I popped my pistol as I broke running through the back parking lot. I could feel and hear bullets flying past my damn head and ears, and I cursed myself for not riding with my first mind with bucking on all meetings. I rushed through a dirt trail pathway, leaving my car behind me. I fired two more shots, still listening to the catastrophe erupt behind me. Jumping over tree logs and a few large ditches, I came out on the following street on the opposite side. As soon as my face protruded from the woods, a pistol was raised to my face by a man I'd never viewed in my life. My instincts were so shaken that I immediately reached for it.

Boom! Boom!

The struggle that we were engaging in with each other caused the gun to fire off, but I couldn't die this way.

He rammed his fist into my jaw forcefully, but I wasn't about to let go of the gun. Shooting him a hard elbow to the gut, his grip on the gun released, and I didn't think again before raising that bitch and putting a slug in his face.

Boom!

His lifeless body dropped hard to the concrete, and it took me a second to regain my breath. I jolted my head around back-and-forth, making sure no one else was trying to take me down. I had to make it out of the area, and I meant quick.

The small apartment complex that rested in front of me was my rescue because I spotted a woman stepping out of her car. Closing the distance took less than one minute, and before she knew it, I was up on her ass.

"Bitch, get the fuck out the way!" I pointed the gun, forcing her to take off running.

Jumping inside the four door Honda, I reversed it out of the lot and headed straight back for the district. I'd just watched Polar get his shit popped for being in the wrong place and not listening. I was going to win and take Rude Boy down myself. The best benefit was I didn't have to share it with anyone. *I'm gonna run Atlantastan,* I thought to myself before placing a call on my cell.

LO

District 1

My patience was wearing thin on hearing an answer back from Taki, and from the looks of her foolishness, it seemed as if she had a different agenda as well. It had been days since she reported back, and the whereabouts of my little brother, JoJo, was igniting the anger in my father as the hours passed. I was selecting a group of individuals to go out and force him back. After the safety of JoJo was secured, I wanted the entire District 7 and 10 obliterated and restructured with true leaders that respected my codes and ethics for Atlantastan.

Stepping into my father and mother's penthouse suite, they

both sat at the table, enjoying lunch together, but the tension was beyond thick. I was sure of one thing. I didn't fail when it came down to making them proud, and I wasn't about to start now. There was a reason I ran District 1. This was my city, and I was willing to show and prove.

Pulling out a chair, I unbuttoned my suit jacket, taking a seat. My mother looked down at her plate, not even addressing me, as if I wasn't there. I didn't blame her. I cut my eyes to my father, and he placed his fork down before intertwining his fingers together.

"My time is so short, son. Since you and your brother was born, my only mission was to keep your lives intact to keep our legacy pumping through these lands. We come from a family of leaders, politicians, and rulers that were always at the top. Are you gonna let us fall any lower?"

I gathered my thoughts, grabbing the bottle of Dalmore L'anima whiskey. I poured myself a drink and tossed it back immediately.

"I'll die before we fall," I said with assurance.

"Indeed you will." He shook his head.

"Listen, Dad, this city isn't big enough for deceit or outlaws. If JoJo isn't returned by tomorrow, our workers will go find him, and I will not allow the bloodshed to stop until I know that all of the perpetrators are spirits. I don't want to risk him. This guy is different, but I need your trust to let me handle this."

"We haven't seen your brother since he was sixteen. He

was lost in these same streets that I allowed you to construct. We're falling from the fate of our own laws, and it's hard to break away laws that people tend to follow and break for so long. I just want my son back," he stressed, lighting his cigar.

"I will say this. I can admit that my hand has slacked a bit to not see something so insidious creeping in our backdoor. I accept it fully but remember that you didn't pick me to run this city for no reason, Dad. You have bigger tables to sit at, and I will back you by enforcing the table you allowed me to sit at. All of these idiots are on borrowed time, but there is one problem that we have with this guy. He's getting help from a known problem that hasn't been in this city for over a decade."

"The name?"

"Ghost."

I could see the look on his face fade nearly to a gloomy grey. He wanted to speak, but his words were jumbled as he forced out his statement.

"Chance Grey."

"Yes, and for some reason, he's helping Rude Boy with this incident, and he is known to be a problem. I have to take the advice of associates when speaking on this man because the word is, he doesn't stop until everybody is resting underneath. I refuse to see this spiral back on you and Mom, so I'm beefing up security for the home. I'm linking districts to annihilate whatever necessary, and I will bring JoJo back home."

"I guess we'll see, won't we?

Rude Boy

THE NIGHT HAD BEEN WILD, AND OF COURSE I ADDED A FEW more bodies on my list because I felt that my crew was being taken for granted. I held the throne when it came to going against opposition, and I still had yet to let up. I wouldn't stop until my woman was back in my grasp. She was my fucking heartbeat, and without her, I was just a monster. I called a meet up in my district, down in the Campbellton Road plaza. I owned a few stores, and all the territory made it easy to stamp my position throughout the city.

"I'm doing my best to end this shit, and I just wanna let everybody know that I appreciate all of you for standing beside me for Shanti," I voiced.

"No thanks over here. This is what I do." Ghost shrugged, still texting on his cell.

"Yeah, as long as I'm getting paid, it's respect. I mean business is business, so me and my crew standing." Seven spoke up as he stood next to Dahlia and his crew.

JoJo, quiet as always, just glared around at us all, and I knew that he was taking this shit we had going on more than hard. His polluted minded brother felt that just because we were living in the most violent times of the city that he needed to enforce violence against everyone instead of when necessary. I intended to kill him so quickly and place all of this bullshit behind me because I knew he wouldn't stop. That included killing Daffy. He had at least six bullets coming to his skull, and it was well deserved. I'd never seen his filthy side coming, but it wasn't surprising. I was going to play my cards right until Shanti was back with me, then all these transgressors would be a dead memory.

"So, how do you expect to get this girl back? We need to think of something quick because bloodshed is only gonna heighten things. You have to move smooth and take the correct steps cause this ain't the average situation where a few dead bodies can straighten everything," Ghost questioned with curiosity on his expression.

"I'm being as careful as possible, and my plan has to be natural, just like the way we moving now. Planning shit will only crash because you can't plot on killing an entire city that's already dead. Any district could be aiming at us after this, let alone tomorrow is the deadline for JoJo to cut ties with my crew, and from the statements he been making, it don't look like he separating himself from me no time soon. I can't go no other way but forward because it damn sho coming at us," I replied before lighting a cigarette.

As I inhaled the nicotine, I didn't even get the chance to blow out the smoke before hearing the sounds of handguns racking back.

"Hey, everybody, hands the fuck up! FBI and don't make me fucking say it again!" the officer yelled, pointing the gun sternly at us all.

We all remained still, and I could feel the tension go from one hundred to a million with the disrespect from the authorities in my own district. I knew that whatever he had on his mind, it wasn't going to go as planned. The expression on Ghost, JoJo, Dahlia, and Seven's faces changed immediately.

"You got to be the dumbest cracker in the academy to be trimming around my territory at night alone. Now, I don't know if you think we're some ordinary jokers, but I know you will not complete whatever mission you came to pursue. You may wanna turn and leave," I warned, pulling on my cigarette again.

"Mr. Khalifa Bah, trust me, you're not going unnoticed, and you can bet your ass I'm not here for no reason. I'll wait to mention the criminal record you're building every hour on the street, but you got a visitor with you that's been wanted for a long time with my force, and I'm not leaving without you sons of bitches in cuffs. Now, put your hands up and slowly get on the ground. All of you." He kept his eye trained on Ghost.

I exhaled and put my hands up, and just as I went to kneel, two gunshots rang out loudly.

Bloc! Bloc!

The first slug struck the dirty ass Fed in the center of the head, sending his blood across the parking lot, and the second crashed into his chest cavity. He was knocked off his feet, and I knew that he was dead before his body collapsed into the concrete.

"What the fuck was that?! We don't kill officers down here, Dahlia. You just erupted a whole alarm in my district. Now we got more than some fucking enemies to be worried about!" I clenched my jaws tight in anger.

Dahlia still held her gun, not caring for an excuse, and we all immediately started to scramble to exit the scene.

"He was pointing a fucking gun at us. What else was I supposed to do cause, clearly, y'all was about to let us die, Daddy?" She rushed over toward her car.

I didn't even have the words to give her at the moment. Me and JoJo wasted no time climbing into my Dodge Challenger SRT, and I glanced around, confused, for a second.

"Where the fuck did Ghost go?" I cut my eyes to JoJo.

"I watched him walk off when Dahlia shot the cop. He was moving normal, as if it didn't even happen. Even with my eye on him, I still couldn't tell you where he just disappeared to. Where did this guy come from, Rude? He's strange."

"Yeah, you know I'll never speak my energy out loud, but I can agree. Let's just hope he will meet us at the safe spot because something's telling me the house is not gonna be comfortable for a few weeks." I mashed the gas pedal, speeding from the shopping plaza down Delowe Drive.

The death of a cop was bad business, and I knew for a fact that the streets of District 7 were about to be flooded with a ton of these bitches by morning. I couldn't afford a war with the government and the dictator of Atlanta. I needed Shanti back, so I could end this shit for good. Judging from what just happened, the help of Agent Porter may be out the window. I cursed silently, hoping this didn't flip in our faces. Atlantastan was about to crash down, and I was definitely going with it if I didn't get my wife back in my grasp before it did.

∼

District 6
East Atlanta

I COULDN'T WASTE MY TIME EVEN RESIDING IN MY OWN district after what had just taken place. My limits in this city were wide, but that didn't mean I couldn't get in a bad mix being in the wrong place at the wrong time. I called up a good Cuban friend of Kamo's, who was an enforcer for District 5, and he welcomed us into his territory with open arms. The eastside was broken down into a few districts, but the share that my associate controlled accumulated the most money. Our destination ended up being a five-bedroom home with a gated entrance wrapped around the entire premises.

Pulling into the parking lot behind Yazi, he shut off his engine and climbed out of the all-white Ferrari Pininfarina he was pushing. He didn't hesitate to push over and greet all of us, and I still had yet to hear from Ghost, and it was as if he'd just evaporated in the air. He was definitely needed and running around the wrong places could easily get him mangled and decapitated if the right hater happened to lay eyes on him.

"Rude Boy, I still can't believe what happened to Sami, and my family is seeking nothing but death for his retribution. The true Cuban way. He always respected you and spoke great about your character, so whatever you need is on me. You can keep the home until everything is over with, but there are a few things that we really need to take care of for the sake of Sami's name. The Mexicans out in the upper district have totally rebelled against paying the debts owed to my uncle, and the business that we both participate in today is the reason why we earn the caliber of currency that we do. I'm not sure how their leader is willing to handle this, but that retribution must be paid in full," he stressed.

"Consider it done, whatever it takes. I appreciate the assistance, and we won't be here too long to overburden you. My word, mon." I shook his hand with assurance.

"Perfect. I'll let you guys be, and I guess we can talk tomorrow. Whatever you need is inside. Stay dangerous, Rude Boy," he stated before tossing the house keys in my hand.

"Of course." I nodded, watching him climb back in this million-dollar car. He sped out of the gate, leaving us to ourselves, and the time to sit and properly plan was now. I needed Shanti back, and I needed to do it quickly, so I wouldn't have any remorse killing these fucking clowns. The only thing I could do was sit back and wait for Agent Porter to show up with a hell storm behind her partner getting murdered. Physically, she couldn't say that we did anything, but running the entire District 7 was enough guilt alone. I didn't need to be at odds with this bitch.

"We need to head in and talk because after tonight, everything that we're gonna do will be for a purpose. We don't have much time, and I know we have to strike fast, or all this shit is about to crumble up on us."

I stopped before saying what was on my mind next because the silhouette of a man walking up the driveway caught my eye. He wore a black hoodie, and it clearly wasn't a shadow playing tricks on me. I pulled my gun as did Seven and Dahlia. It wasn't until he got close enough that I realized it was this crazy ass nigga, Ghost. He was just walking around as if there wasn't a whole war at hand.

"What the fuck, my nigga? Where the fuck did you disappear to?" I gave him a strange look to peep his energy.

"Nigga, do I look like the fucking police? While others waste time, I disperse as if I was never there. It's the way I been moving around this city, my boy. Remember that I'm born and raised here." He smirked, walking toward the house.

I shook my head, knowing that he was definitely an asshole, but his energy gave me the light that said he was standing behind the shit that I was on, and I needed him at the moment.

"Wassup with your peoples?" Seven tapped my shoulder, whispering lightly.

"I don't see anything wrong. The nigga is just confident as

a motherfucker. Seems like that's what we need right now. Just relax." I tapped his shoulder, quickly dismissing his statement.

Heading inside, my mind contemplated on how I was making my next checkmate on this bitch, Taki, and placing her ass exactly where she needed to be. Right after that, I would make my way for Lo, and after business was solidified, I was getting the fuck away from the city no matter where I migrated. It was time to start over.

AGENT JAMIYAH PORTER

Federal Building
Downtown Atlanta

I t was seven forty-five in the morning, and I was sitting in the corner of my boss' office, crying my heart out about my partner, Agent Lace. The emotions erupted in me even more when I found out that he was killed inside of Rude Boy's district. I knew for a fact that he carried the power of anything that took place in that area because no one moved an inch without adding his name in the middle. I was fuming heavily, and my only thought was on addressing him and getting down to who the fuck did it. Another officer of the law was taken down by the hands of a filthy ass criminal. If Rude

Boy even slightly knew what had occurred, the entire agreement was off, and I was going to be sure to toss all of his little flunkies in the bottom of a penitentiary right next door to him.

"Agent Porter, I need to speak with you alone please," my chief and commander requested as the meeting was dismissed.

I didn't have the energy to talk or debate, but I was willing to hear whatever he needed to say. A former agent was now dead, and I felt more than horrible that I wasn't beside him to at least assist. That was the only question that continued to pick at my brain. Why was Lace alone in District 7 after hours? It didn't make sense.

Walking behind my boss into the hallway corridor, he allowed our co-workers to disperse before facing me.

"Hey, I know you're probably a little jumbled in the head about Lace. I know he was a great partner, and honestly, I'm glad that it wasn't you. These districts that we deal with are not our land, but we govern the land around it to ensure that the people know we still have a hold over this state. Yes, this is our career, but we also have a set structure on how we do things so mistakes like this won't occur. We're gonna send out the force on a daily patrol, and we all know how dangerous this is. Lace was one of us, and I want whoever is responsible. You allow the force to work and snatch up as many of these guys as they can and play the back field. Do your homework and stay on the safe side until we clear these assholes from the street. This call is far beyond my head, but it's the best that I can do for now," he explained with empathy in his tone.

"The back field, sir? I mean, with all respect, sir, this was my partner for the past three years, a great agent that sacrificed time and his life to protect this contaminated city. We should be eliminating these threats the same way. My partner is dead, and he lost his life on the front field. How can I honor him standing back and acting as if the force will accomplish anything behind that?"

"Porter, your pain is clear and evident, but the only thing that a happen right now is you putting your own life at risk and even worse, this entire department. We have to think beyond the criminal, not like them. If I could put a bullet in Lace's killer's head, I wouldn't hesitate one second. I have a job description to follow as well, and that's following the orders of the superiors."

"Let me guess, the senator of state? You know just like I do that he's more crooked than half of the thugs we chase away for a living. His son literally is the reason this city is lost in death and corruption. We've heard the accusations…"

"Yes, we have, and we also don't go off accusations. We go off proof, Agent Porter. Now, I know you're highly upset, but don't go against the ruling on our oaths. It'll take time, but we will handle this. I'm ordering you to just do your job. Don't chase down what hasn't come to you. Leave this situation to the higher administration and leave Khalifa Bah for the force," he stated with a serious face.

"Khalifa Bah? Rude Boy? Why did you mention him? I've never said anything about him," I asked curiously.

"The office talks, Porter. The streets talk as well, and he keeps appearing across my desk. I'm only telling you to let this happen the correct way. Don't rush yourself into taking anybody down and falling in the same motion. I only give you this advice because of how hard your principles stand out as an agent. You're one of the best but don't forget that we're all dispensable," he said before leaving me in my own thoughts.

I didn't know exactly what was going on, but something was telling me that it wasn't right. I had too much experience in my field, and allowing Lace to lose his life without risking mine to get the one responsible wouldn't even sit right in my chest. I was more than capable of taking care of myself, and I was going to use the same streets to get justice for my partner.

Heading toward the front of our building, I made my way to the parking lot and tried to dial Rude Boy's number. When I didn't get an answer, I climbed inside my car to track his ass down. There were answers that I needed, and for some reason, I knew he had them.

I made my way out of the department's parking lot and headed straight for District 7.

∼

Daffy

IT WASN'T EVEN TWENTY-FOUR HOURS THAT HAD PASSED before I made the step I needed to rise above everybody that held any position with the Kiss Squad. After the close encounter with Rude Boy and Polar's death, it had me moving more strategically with this retarded ass Jamaican. He was invincible, but I tipped the hat to where it was meant. He was far from slow.

After making a phone call, I found myself pulling up in District 1 to Lo's office. It was far different from our neck of the woods, and anybody couldn't just show up unannounced to the property. The place was heavily guarded. Once I parked my car and stepped out, I was immediately approached by a few men that were casually dressed in all-black. I nearly reached for my gun, but the guard who was closest to me shook his head.

"You wouldn't even have a chance to pull it, sir. Lo's been expecting you. This way." He motioned for me to follow. I quickly brushed off the remark, knowing that I needed this shot at winning this city, and once the ball was in my court, I was doing more than taking advantage.

After being escorted to his office, they allowed me to walk in alone. Lo sat at his desk, peacefully scanning whatever paperwork that laid in front of him. I took his quietness as business and just took a seat.

"It's nice that you're here. I mean, I don't usually care for certain people stepping foot across that office threshold, but you, on the other hand, are different." He spoke, still with his attention on the papers.

"Yeah, I would feel that way too when I look at me. I

wouldn't be here if I wasn't a man you cared for stepping through here. Surely I'm gonna show my efforts once I find out what's next. I wanna eat. I wanna be king. I'll do anything I have to for it," I replied humbly.

Raising his vision, he matched my stare. I could see that he was trying to read me, and I couldn't say that I didn't want him to. Lo was the biggest supplier, murderer, and dictator in Atlanta, and he only built relationships for one reason. More power.

"Understood." He nodded. "This is much bigger and personal to me, so I stand clear and direct on what I need. I'm a businessman and also an executor with my words. District 7 is the definition of innovation, the group of society that doesn't want to abide by rules of life. It's a mockery of my family, all the foundations we've built, the organizations we started, the lives we placed into position. Their rebellious conditions makes it all worth nothing. Now, I have to make examples."

"I'm listening."

"Rude Boy needs to die. I want him mutilated and deleted from my city. Anything related to him. My only concern is losing my brother, JoJo, in the process. He must not be touched. So, carefully delete the necessary pieces to make it as easy as possible. I'll make you very rich and a hand of power in this city, but this must not fail. Bring my brother to me and District 7 is yours and whatever else you could possibly think of."

"That's understood, but it's more to me than just District 7. I wanna run the entire Kiss Squad through every district. No, it won't be to undercut on any businesses or leaders but more like an enforcement for you that'll always be able to take care of any problem, any time. I can push your muscle around this entire city, and you can kick your feet back," I offered.

His face said that I was pushing the bar, but after a few seconds, his energy loosened before holding his hand out.

"Deal and that's sealed."

His motherfucking grip was a little firm for a skinny white man. It was the posture and the energy that allowed me to know he was nothing to be played with. I also had a side of me that stood on business, so it was mutual.

"Deal."

As I made my way out of his office, I took note to myself that from that day on, I was unleashing the bullshit, and murder was just much too simple.

∼

Rude Boy
Safe House
District 6

I HAD JUST WOKEN ALMOST AN HOUR AGO AND WAS ALREADY networking with other districts about the move I was about to make. I couldn't sit any longer waiting for Lo's havoc to fall, and neither was I about to keep wasting time when I'd heard Shanti's desperate voice. I was about to pull whatever necessary starting today. I had a large catered lunch privately delivered to the home for the small crew I had working with me. There were some of the best Jamaican dishes and expensive filets with shrimp. I needed to acknowledge the fact that these individuals stood beside me without any rebuttal of my situation. There were a few disagreements, but we were holding it together. This shit was bound to get out of hand, and most of us would surely succumb to the curse of this city, but it was for a purpose.

After eating, we all sat at the table, discussing the next move and how I would proceed from that day on out. I stressed about the safety issue and also the fact that everyone's family would receive all benefits if anything were to happen. Ghost, along with a few of the Cali crew, was onboard. JoJo was at my side as always, and Seven was out checking in on all close associates.

"We leave this bitch at sun fall, and we're just gonna keep mashing the gas until this smoke clears. I want Shanti back at any cost. I thank you all."

I thought that my conscience was playing tricks on me because I saw the gun in my peripheral. I noticed it was Agent Porter aiming her gun directly at me. Everyone else was slow to move except JoJo. He pulled his strap, and she still didn't budge. Everyone else remained calm when I raised my hand.

"Is there any reason why you're invading this private property, Agent Porter? You know there is a proper way to enter a fucking home." I mugged her.

"Fuck you. You're a dirty criminal that I should've killed long ago for the sake of this community. You're better off dead. Cop killer!" she spat back, inching toward me.

"Well, if you feel that way, pull the trigger, Ms. Porter. I've given nothing but sincerity and life to this dead ass city, and now something valuable to me has been taken. I'll do all necessary to gain that back, but I will never kill a fucking cop, no matter how much I hate your kind. Now you can kill me, and you'll die maybe a half a second later, or you can calm down and allow me to help get rid of the one who's your real problem." I tried to bargain.

I knew her pride and oath to the agency was something she'd die for, but my request was one that she had to respect as the truth.

I watched her face fidget with anger before she lowered the gun, exhaling deeply.

"We do this starting now. I want the idiot that killed my partner, and after all this is over with, when this person that's so-called responsible meets justice, you better pray you've made it so far away from this country that Jesus himself wouldn't be able to find you. We need to talk in private," she demanded before walking back out of my dining area.

JoJo lowered his pistol, and everyone started to rush with their opinions. I immediately held up a hand, quieting them.

Looking at Ghost, he nodded, and I was assured nothing would get out of hand.

I casually walked out of the home, and she was standing with her arms folded, facing the exit. Closing the door behind me, I thought carefully before I spoke.

"I just wanna let you know I'm not your enemy here."

"I'm starting not to know who my enemy is. I became a protector for the government for a reason. My partner was the exact same. I'm tired of chasing the fish when I can just drain the entire sea and kill this nonsense for good. You know who murdered him the same way I have info on where Shanti may be held. It looks like we both are on a personal mission now."

I grew angry just listening, but Shanti was my wife and literally the missing piece to me and her entire family. I needed her back and safe. Then, I was going to finish these other liabilities for good.

"I think you need to go ahead and explain what's next because we will get nowhere going back-and-forth. It's understood. Now, what's next?"

"We need to get to upper district. Gwinett County."

"The Mexicans?"

She nodded her head, and I immediately understood what the next task was. I was about to wipe the entire upper district off the map to find Shanti.

∼

ATLANTASTAN 2

Taki

I HAD BEEN DOING A LOT OF PLOTTING TO GET MY MIND prepared for this war against Rude Boy. I was pushing the issue on my team reigning this city, and all I needed was him to oblige and stand beside me like a best friend was supposed to. No one liked to lose anything, but if a battle wasn't fought wholeheartedly, it was already lost before it was started. I was just a bitch who couldn't take those losses.

Parking my car, I stepped out and looked across the street at the small shop. Traffic was moving about freely, and I was far from out of place in District 7. I blended in so well that I knew that I would complete my mission with ease. I only had one set agenda — make Rude Boy suffer and eventually vow down his power and love strictly to me.

I strolled casually across the street and made my way inside. Rude Boy's aunt stood behind the counter, straightening a few records that were on the shelves, and some young guy that was posted along the side of her assisted. It was a face that I wasn't familiar with. I applied the lock on the door without being noticed and made my way to the counter.

"Hello, Taki, how are you, precious? Long time no hear." She smiled at me.

"Hey, queen. It has been a minute and may be even longer after this time. Honestly, I just came to ask you a question."

"Shoot away, darling."

"Have you heard anything from Khalifa lately? He has

been real distant since Shanti left, and I just wanted to know if he was okay."

"Oh, my child, he is so distraught right now. I begged my nephew to leave this country, to just try and find himself. I spoke with him yesterday, and he mentioned being out in District 6. Trying to rebuild for a second, I guess."

The one statement she mentioned allowed me to know that he was working with the Cubans, obviously Sami's circle. There wasn't many places to hide in this city without me knowing, and I was always a step ahead. I could see the young individual with her eyeing me with suspicion, and I didn't have time to waste or any room to leave more hurdles in my objective.

"Well, at least he's trying. It's been a while since I've heard some great reggae. Is it possible this young cutie right here can find me something fresh on the shelf?" I asked to distract her.

"Sure, gal. Honey, be a dear and hand me a few reggae demos if you will." She touched his shoulder.

He stared me down once more before turning to complete her request. I reached directly into my bag, pulling the small 9mm from my Gucci purse. Without hesitation, I raised it to the back of his head and pulled the trigger.

Boom!

His blood and skull splattered across the CDs and tapes before he collapsed to the floor.

Rude Boy's aunt froze in shock and could barely utter a sound until I pointed the gun directly in between her eyes.

"Oh, my! God is the most merciful. Taki, whyyy? When have me ever done you any wrong, eh?" She spoke softly, still glancing at the body in front of her.

"Well, times have changed, beautiful, and trust me, I've always liked you, but your nephew has stepped out of bounds, and regardless of how much love we share, he has to know that when trouble dismembers the same love, emotions become empty as the midnight sky. Sorry, beautiful." I raised the gun and placed one bullet to her chest.

Boom!

The shop grew quiet, and I walked around the counter to search for exactly what I needed. Once I located her cell phone, I began to scroll through it swiftly. It didn't take long for me to find exactly what I was looking for. I smiled before I placed it in my bag and exited the store. It was time to show the true demon within me. I was coming for everything.

RUDE BOY

Upper District
Gwinnett County

Gathering up my team, along with the psychotic woman, Agent Porter, we made our way to the upper district to handle the affair for Yazi but also the new information that had been given to her from the federal informant, Tizo. The Mexicans were a part of a large branch in Atlantastan. They were mainly involved in the human trafficking lane, along with dealing bricks of methamphetamine. They murdered for the will of Lo and Sami, but after the death of my associate, things had spiraled out of control.

We were all posted in three separate cars along the side of the road. I made sure that we did our best to blend in with the district because it was so easy to be noticed. My idea was to go ahead and eliminate everyone in front of the workshop until we found our way inside, but of course Agent Porter felt that she had a better chance of getting in without causing too much of a disturbance. I watched as she made her way across the street, and just as I suspected, the henchmen for the dope house began to get a little crazy when they surrounded her dumb ass. I warned her not to make the cop move and feel that these crazy ass Hispanics would spare her.

Me and my team wasted no time falling out of the cars quickly. Our guns were already aimed, and before they noticed us approaching, Ghost fired his gun, striking one of them in the head.

Boc!

It didn't take long for an all-out war to break out in the middle of the street. I was the first to reach Agent Porter and snatch her ass up to her feet.

"I fucking told you!"

"Now is not the time, just shut up and follow me!" she shouted back as we ran for cover.

Boc! Boc! Boc! Pak! Pak! Bak! Bak!

My team traded fire with the Mexicans, and I could tell just from how their men were dropping that they may not have enough security for the district. It gave us a major advantage, but we had yet to see how this shit was about to turn out in the home.

Me and Agent Porter made our way on the side of the house, and she took the lead, kicking in the door. Crossing the threshold, she fired a shot, killing another guard instantly.

Boc!

I kept my gun raised, not knowing if another motherfucka would be jumping from around the corner, and once I laid eyes on my target, Carlos, I pointed my gun directly at his forehead.

"If you move, I'll blow yo shit to pieces, pussy!"

"Whoa, whoa! You muthafuckas come in my territory, killing my fucking men. This is not legit. It's not legit at all. What the fuck is this about?" He stretched his hands in the air out of fear of being shot.

"We'll be the ones asking the questions, idiot. Now, I surely didn't come all this way for nothing." Agent Porter flashed her badge to him.

"What the fuck? You're a cop? Rude Boy, you're working with the people? I can only imagine what will happen to you when Lo finds out about this!" he threatened indirectly.

She slammed her gun into his mouth, causing his blood to pour profusely.

"We're not into the word battling right now because you might not be able to say a word to Lo if my question doesn't get answered. I'm sure the name Tizo finds you very well. He's your cousin, right, because that's how I'm standing in your establishment as we speak?" She gazed down at him as

I crept through the small home, looking for any trace of Shanti.

I moved around every inch of the house and still came up empty-handed, so I knew there was more treacherous shit to come in order to snatch her back.

Making my way back to the entry area, Agent Porter still held her position.

"I'll ask you one time and one time only. We know that Taki is backing this district with money and product. We also know that she's the one behind Shanti's disappearance. Tell us where the girl is, and we'll leave. You won't have to suffer like the rest of your friends outside."

I looked up at Ghost and JoJo stepping through the door, guns up. I raised my hand, forcing them to pause. I needed to see if Agent Porter could get what I so badly needed out of this man.

"Taki is not gonna let you get away with any of this. Tizo will face his fate. The Kiss Squad has their hands in everything around this city, and I don't know if you heard, but you're not gonna be able to walk around none of these districts without a red dot being placed on your head!" he shouted.

He shifted his vision back-and-forth between us as if he wanted to buck, but I could tell he knew that things were going to turn bad if he didn't oblige.

"Taki is holding her somewhere out in District 5. She's working with my cousin, man. Him and your slime ball friend, K-roc. He's been giving her intel on your district, and Mendez still wants blood from the last war you guys just unleashed on our people. Tizo is gonna die, and it's no fucking way you can stop it. Getting what the fuck I'm saying now, chica?" He stared up at us from the floor.

I stepped in front of Agent Porter, pressing my sneaker against his throat.

"We can stop it. You just should of wished you wasn't a part of it." I raised my burner, shooting him in the face twice.

Boom! Boom!

"Hey! You still remember that this is my call. He could've gotten us closer alive." She pushed my shoulder.

I clenched my jaws, stepping up into her personal space.

"Fuck that! He gave us all we need. We have to rethink this shit and come correct. You're a cop at the end of the day, and you may know Atlantastan, but you don't know the inside of the districts like I do, so you ain't got no choice but to follow my lead."

She didn't back down, but I could tell I humbled her a bit.

"Aye, we need to get the hell outta here. You two can fuck later on." Ghost cut in before dispersing from the home.

I knew that she wanted to say more, but we couldn't sit in the same spot too long. Eventually, Lo would get the word, and a clean-up crew would be on every corner of this city.

Exiting the premises, I viewed the disaster that covered the streets, and more blood was guaranteed to be shed. Snakes slithered around my domain at will, and K-roc's disappearance made much sense. My mind started to work in overload, and in my heart, I knew that my girl was inside the territory of Mendez's operation. I was prepared to die, and by morning, I was anticipating the end when I pushed down in his residence.

Climbing inside our cars, we sped away from our location, heading back to District 6.

∼

Lo
District One
Midtown Lofts

I WAS SITTING IN THE DINING ROOM OF MY LOFT AT THE LARGE, glass, marble table with four other special people in my corner. When I was in need, they would come. When I had troubles getting rid of a pest, they never failed. My connections allowed me to purchase four of the best trained killers in the entire south, and I was about to let them all feast.

When the hands on my Audemars Piguet watch stood tall on the twelve, indicating it was midnight, I cleared my throat before I spoke.

"It's been a great minute since I've had this sort of sit down with you all, and I hate to have pulled you in at such short notice, but I had no option. My father's requesting that this is urgent and has no limits to whatever needs to be met for it to be. You all will be compensated in full, that including property so you're able to expand financially. All districts are on alert of your arrival, so if anyone stands in the way, you can eliminate whomever you wish." I rotated my head, locking eyes with them all.

"So, who is this lucky person, me friend?" Di'meech asked in his Italian accent. He was a nasty young man with a smart mind for executing. He was big in every major city, as were the other three. There was Lara from the Bronx, a Spanish plug's daughter that had a taste for blood, Ken from Atlantastan originally, a cutthroat serial killer that did heists for a living, and last but not least, there was Whisper, an ex-cop that had been on the run since the early 2000s for multiple homicides. It was a treacherous crew that didn't have boundaries.

"His name is Rude Boy. I think you all are quite familiar with this rising star of our city. His weight has grown too big for his shoes, and it needs to be reduced immediately. The only pass is for my brother, JoJo, so you snatch him however you have to and finish it off when he is secured. Force him if you have to. If he tries to run off with this traitor and innovator, kill him," I said with a straight face before pouring a glass of Remy Martin champagne.

I made my way around the table, filling them all a glass.

"Toast to getting wealthy and business. If anything isn't understood, please speak your peace." I gave a wry smile, concealing my anger.

The peaceful opera music from my home system played

gently in the background, and just like always, I didn't receive any objections. I shrugged, raising my glass.

"To business." We all spoke in unison before tossing back the expensive drink.

"This should be fun. I haven't been to this little town in a while, ya heard. So, I'll be killing me a bundle and trying to find one of these trill south niggas to fuck on for this short vacation break." Lara laughed, pouring herself another glass.

"I agree. I'm familiar with Rude Boy. He's always been straight forward with me, but business is far more straight in my mental. Still not too fond of personal work," Di'meech voiced, lighting his cigar.

"Nothing personal, just business. We've never saw the good in a soul before taking it any other time, and he is no different," I chimed back in sternly.

"Well, it looks like we got hunting to do." Whisper spoke.

"So it seems. Please have fun." I nodded before taking my seat.

AGENT JAMIYAH PORTER

Safe House
District 6

I was back in the walls of Rude Boy's hideout, plotting how I would take down the head of this city's trouble with a bunch of criminals. The house was guarded by six men, and I felt awkward sitting in the same room as a bunch of coldblooded killers. It didn't move me because I wouldn't hesitate to sign one of their spirits away to God, but this asshole, Rude Boy, worked on my mind since he'd disrespected me in front of his little buddies. The way he stared at me gave me goosebumps but made me horny in the same motion. I hated a drop-dead handsome lawbreaker, let alone a smart ass. I needed Lace's murderer, but I also wanted to know where the root of this evil rested, so I could cast it out for good.

I was occupying a guest room right down the hall from his, and I needed to speak my mind while all his little flunkies were scattered around the house, resting up. I stood up and checked myself in the mirror before leaving the room. The hallway was enormous, decked with expensive cherry oak floors and extraordinary flowers and vases. I walked slowly down the hall that led to his room and noticed that the door was cracked.

I didn't want to look like I was spying, but I was still a whole agent running through a criminal's hideout. Taking a step in, I noticed him lying back on the bed in a pair of basketball shorts, his gun resting right beside him. I couldn't tell if he was asleep because of the dreadlocks covering his face, but when he spoke, I clearly received my answer.

"Is there a reason you creeping in my room, three in the morning, Agent Porter?" He still laid motionless.

I wrapped my arms around my chest, gathering my answer in my head, because truly there were all kinds of reasons.

"I wanna know what's this big ass plan you got to end all this? How do I know you're gonna even do right and help me after you get your little lovebird back?"

The rain that had been pouring since earlier started to pour harder, and a loud thundering erupted as he sat up slowly in the bed. Shit really gave me the creeps, but I was too curious to move. The dark room casted his vision and face as he made his way over to me, once again closing that distance, like what had given me the bubble guts earlier.

"All you have to do is follow, and if you have doubts on trusting me, you can just leave and proceed how you please. My word is my word."

"You know, for someone that caused half of this torment in the city, you sure do have a lot of arrogance with it lately, like you could just snap your finger. You have a mission and so do I, and I don't intend on failing, so I need to know a plan. I wouldn't be standing in your bedroom late in the night if I didn't."

He titled his head, smirking at me.

"Or maybe you would be standing here. I see the way you look at me, Agent Porter. It seems like you are dedicated to your job for sure, but I also see the urge to want to be a part of something. I catch you staring at me, gazing with confusion in your eyes on my world. In reality, you wish you could taste my reality and still hold your oath to make you feel righteous. When in reality, you just wanna be loved and respected. That's why you go so hard trying to stop us. So we can feel like you." He took another step up on me.

His chest was touching my elbow, and I could feel his muscles tensing up under his tank top. In a way, he was so right. He was a dream man in my eyes — his looks, his business savvy. His dark but mesmerizing pupils always made me slightly moist, and I hated to admit it . I was caging in feeling for a fool that I wouldn't hesitate to take down just a few weeks back. I immediately started to hate his ass at that moment, putting me on blast like he'd read my mental.

"Fuck you, Rude Boy. You don't know me!" I brushed my chest against his with force.

Before I could think of slapping his ass, he leaned in, passionately kissing my lips. His tongue was so tender and delightful sliding between my lips, and I wanted to snatch away to whip my gun out. Instead, my legs grew weak in my knees, and my kitty started to flutter like a hummingbird's wings. Before I knew it, I was mimicking his action, locking lips with my eyes closed.

After my conscience told me to snatch myself from the trap, I fell even more until I couldn't contain my hormones.

Turning around, I placed my plump ass against his midsection, looking back at him. I could feel his manhood pulsating through his shorts, and I was feeling a heart attack approaching in my chest.

Grabbing me slowly around my stomach, he stepped with me over to the bed.

"What the hell are you doing? You can't do nothing like this to me. I'm an officer of the law." I tried to breathe through the lump in my throat.

"You just was in my presence on the wrong night. I see the pain you can't shake, and sometimes we need help breaking it."

Bending me slowly over the bed, my body just naturally

arched to his touch. He unbuttoned my black khaki pants and removed my gun holster, tossing it aside. I moaned lightly in anticipation. Pulling down my pants, he stared at my round backside, rubbing it like a soft pillow. I watched his shorts drop to the floor and gasped wondering what the hell I had just gotten myself into. Licking his palm, he massaged it across my pussy, sending me into ecstasy immediately. He eyed me like prey, rotating his hand back-and-forth. Stroking his dick behind me, he slid slowly into my treasure chest, setting off my adrenaline. His first few strokes were mid paced, as if he didn't want to touch me, but right after, he sped up, mashing inside of me like a fun toy.

"Dammnnn!" I moaned lightly, trying not to be loud.

Our eyes never left each other, and after a few minutes of this sick, twisted ass entanglement, we were fucking like we had a score to settle with one another. I knew this was going to go to left field, and I didn't plan on anything different, but tonight we were releasing energy from us both that was obviously long overdue. Tomorrow was a life-or-death moment, so I enjoyed every second I could before my boring ass reality returned.

∼

Taki
District 6

ATLANTASTAN 2

It didn't take me long to find the duck away home that Rude Boy was obviously building a new foundation in. His life was either mine or it was on borrowed time. I arrived in the area around 8:30 that morning, my killers stumbled across the perfect entrance, and I didn't hesitate to make my performance remembered. His associate, Yazi, was pulling out the front gate in his Benz, and my goons didn't hesitate to surround it and aim every gun we owned at each side of his car.

I casually walked across the street, staring at him like a deer in the night, and he was immediately snatched out by my guard, Nino.

"You got to be the dumbest bitch ever to step out here. Your gonna fuc..."

His sentence was cut short from my guys beating him into a quick submission. Within seconds, he was leaking profusely from the face and was barely conscious.

I laughed, twirling in a circle.

"I don't care what district I'm in. I control who dies and who doesn't. I would suppose Rude and a few more are hiding inside?" I asked, looking around at the empty street and neighborhood. We were so quick and silent that no one probably even recognized ten armed men in the streets snatching up another victim.

"Too late, bitch! He's gone and probably heading to where you don't want him. He knows, Taki. We all know!" he spat through his bloody mouth, glaring at me.

"Tear it the fuck down. If he's in there, I want him alive."

My men jumped into action, raiding the property full force. I pulled my 9mm handgun, aiming at Yazi's head.

"I always win, idiot. You're just gonna be another casualty in Rude Boy's dilemma, so I can't say the same for you."

I waited outside the home, and within five minutes, my men were flooding back out.

"It's empty, boss. He's the only one. We searched it up and down."

I immediately felt enraged and crashed the butt of my gun across Yazi's face, shattering his nose.

"Fuckk!" He twirled on the concrete in agony as my men circled us.

"I'll give you one chance to tell me who he's with and where, and you can get out of dodge. If not, you'll live right here forever, and I'll find them the hard way," I offered.

"He's exactly where he needs to be. By the time you get there, he'll be gone again, and everyone in that area will be dead. Suck me, bitch!" He tried to spit on me.

It landed inches away, and I shook my head with pity.

"You're sacrificing yourself, all for him. How pathetic."

"Boss, we can knock these hideouts down brick by brick. It's no point in waiting any longer. He can't get too ahead of us, or we'll be at a disadvantage." My assassin, Nino, handed me the detonator for my grand finale.

I was trying to move in silence until I got my hands on

him, and he was surely going to beg. But Nino was absolutely right. Play time was over.

Exhaling, I smiled and pressed the trigger, watching the small mansion blow to pieces and go up in flames.

Boooooommmmmm!

Scattered debris went flying, and we all turned our heads from the smoke that quickly filled the sky. Waving my hand to clear my vision, I bent down over Yazi.

"Now your district belongs to me, winner. See you in the next life." I removed a four-inch blade from my back and quickly divided his throat in two. I watched him gasp for life, and he was actually a killer that I once respected. That was until he stepped in my business, and it was only getting started.

"Spread out and find these motherfuckers. Now!" My team scattered for their cars, and I looked at my disaster one last time before strolling calmly back to my car. His statement about Rude Boy flowed through my mind slowly, and the thought of his remark forced me to think of the answer to my own question.

"Mendez," I uttered before signaling my men. "Get out to District 5 right now. He's trying to throw our attention. He knows where she is," I ordered before jumping in my driver's seat and smashing off.

Leaving out of the cul-de-sac, Shanti's ugly face popped in my head, and I realized we had been tricked.

Son of a bitch! If I can't have you, she can't, I thought to myself as we all headed for the highway.

~

Shanti

IT HAD BEEN SO LONG SINCE I HAD ANY SIGN THAT I WOULD make it out of my predicament. It had been weeks. I wasn't sure how many, but it felt like eternity had passed by. The love of my life had to be so devastated. After I heard his voice, I lodged that bit of hope that he would actually be able to find me. The crazy bitch, Taki, was the nasty slime behind this entire act, and if he would've listened to me and never trusted her close to our family's structure, I wouldn't be in the hole that I was trying to climb out of.

I wouldn't speak nor would I give them any information on my husband's plans or whereabouts. He was my life, and if it meant me dying for his cause, then I was ready to lay down in my coffin. It scared me even more when I realized that Rude Boy's snake ass friends, K-Roc and Daffy, were playing both sides. It was all for power and money. They never had loyalty from the start, and he trusted these niggas with his soul. I was present when these idiots would show up over to the opposition's district to meet and discuss whatever failed attempt they were planning. I would keep my head down, as if I was sleep or exhausted, but I always caught every word.

Both of these niggas were just kicked back in the living room like the bitches they were, speaking on my nigga, and I prayed with every bone in my body that they got what they deserved. I had been left with K-Roc and Mendez, the head Mexican over the district. Niggas were touching on me, even digging their filthy ass fingers in my pants because I was vulnerable and had no win. It was torture, and my spirit was just screaming for their punk asses to just kill me.

"Aye, yo, that was Taki. She said we might need to secure this bitch up. Somebody probably tipped this nigga, Rude Boy, that this bitch is here."

"You the bitch, nigga!" I spat, giving him the evil eye.

"Fuck you, hoe. Mendez, what the fuck are we doing here? She's on the way."

Mendez jumped up from the table with a gun in his hand and rubbed a hand through his slick hair.

"That's impossible. This is the last place that he would ever suspect, and even if he did, let him come. We will war it out just like last time. I owe him one. We're gonna keep making this money and let Taki run herself dry trying to rip love from out of this punta while we capitalize. It's under control. We have seven men outside. It's four of us here. I got this." He blew him off with an attitude.

Before K-roc could give a reply out of his mouth, the sound of the front door came crashing in from the living room area. We were on the second floor, and it sounded like a fucking box truck had just pushed through the bottom of the home.

He immediately grabbed his gun from the glass table, and the two guards that had been posted with us made their way out of the resting area, running down the stairs. The sound of them yelling, along with a few gunshots, let of immediately.

Boc! Boc! Boc! Boc! Boc! Boc!

I was looking around, nervous as fuck. It was just my luck that these niggas' beef had to come pay a visit when I was already hostage with these fucking clowns. I was just a free kill for the slaughter, and my mind started to race.

Mendez held his gun aimed toward the stairwell, fidgeting, not prepared for what was coming. The house grew silent, and the fear started to linger throughout the room.

Mendez leaned to peek his head out for a better visual, and I watched his skull fly completely off his shoulders.

Pewt!

The sound of the bullet was like a small whistle, and he crashed face first to the floor, soaking in a pool of his own blood.

"Jesus!" I screamed, closing my eyes at the sight.

The bitch boy, K-Roc, began to tremble and rushed behind me, latching on to my hair.

"Rude Boy, I know it's you, motherfucker. You play dumb, and I'll kill this bitch right fucking now! You know I will!" He placed the gun up to my temple.

The silence was still thick, and after a few seconds, I

watched Rude slowly reach the top floor with seven other armed individuals with him. They weren't talking, but they all wore bulletproof vests and aimed a gun. Rude kept his grip on his gun tight as he approached us.

"Oh, my God! Rude, baby!" The tears started to rush down my face at just the sight of him.

"Shanti, stop crying. I got you, baby."

"Stay the fuck back, nigga. Don't tempt me, Rude." K-Roc spoke through clenched jaws.

"You know I really thought that you were my brother. You played it real well but not anymore. Let my girl go and we can meet on another time personally and settle this however you choose to, but she's leaving with me one way or the other," he replied calmly.

"Fuck you, pussy. I slaved for you, sucka. I stayed at the bottom to get you rich, and you picked this bitch over our foundation. I knew it would fall like this, and we would be the ones left while you lived your fuck ass fantasy. You aren't made for leadership, Rude. You gave none of us a choice. Taki isn't gonna stop, neither is Lo. You're in between the darkness, baby boy, and you're gonna get lost in it at all costs. I think you need to take you and your little crew back out that front door, or I'll show you she'll make it to God before you touch her again."

I watched Rude exhale deeply with a nod. He looked me in the eyes with so much love, and when I watched him lower his gun and start to back away, my heart dropped.

"I'll grant that. Do not hurt her!" He spoke while motioning for his crew to retreat back.

"Rude, don't leave me, baby, please!" I screamed.

"He ain't got no choice. Clear the house or I'll pull the trigger now!" K-Roc yelled.

They all started to turn and walk away, and my eyes focused on Rude spinning in the opposite direction. K-Roc was so locked in on him that he never saw the other man alongside my nigga spin back around hastily. His gun was aimed directly at us, and without hesitation, he pulled the trigger.

Boom!

I jumped, releasing a few tears, before I felt K-Roc's grip on my neck loosen. I then heard the sound of his body crumbling to the floor, and I glanced back up to Rude, breathing a huge sigh of relief. My tears started to release, and he quickly came to my side, releasing the restraints from my hands.

"Shanti, are you okay, baby? I got you." He pulled me into his grasp tightly.

"Yes, you came and got me. I knew you loved me." I cried into his chest.

The man that handled the business made his way up to the side of Rude.

"We have to leave now, Rude." He spoke with urgency.

"Yeah, I'm glad to see you two reunited, but we don't have a good time frame right about now," a brown skinned woman with an FBI vest on added in.

Rude Boy grabbed my hand, holding me close to him.

"Let's go. We'll talk when we get in a safer area," he agreed, rushing us out of the home as quickly as possible.

When we reached the parking lot, I looked around at the men scattered around lifelessly on the concrete. Bullet holes were all around the home, and it looked as if an all-out army came through implementing Marshall Law. As we all crossed the street toward the parked cars, a line of vehicles were flushing down the street, directly toward us.

"Oh, shit!" He hurried me into the passenger seat. "Listen, baby, JoJo will take you to our safe zone, and I will be there. I need you out of here now. I love you." He kissed my lips, nodding to his killer who rushed to the driver's seat.

"Rude, let's just go, baby. You don't…"

"I do. Trust me." He slammed the door and immediately began to shoot with a few more of his steppers.

JoJo smashed the gas, racing off, and one of the cars with my man's guards followed closely behind.

The sounds of gunshots could be heard as we turned the first corner, evacuating the district. All I could think about was me being rescued to see him risk himself even more. It left me more than worried. I was truly terrified on how this was about to turn out.

TAKI

Arriving in Mendez's district, I sped my BMW down his street and saw Rude Boy and his security exiting my worker's home. I could clearly see bodies lying in the middle of the street, and just viewing the bitch, Shanti, alone placed so much evil into my soul that I nearly wrecked.

Smashing on my brakes, the rest of my crew followed suit, and we all jumped out with our guns blazing.

Boom! Boom! Poc! Poc! Poc! Poc! Poc!

Bullets began to fly instantly, and the bitch, Shanti, was speeding away from my confinement, forcing me to lose my leverage. Rude Boy and a few of his men scattered around, returning fire, as if the war was more than understood.

I watched my gun take one of his men's head clean off, but they still banged it out heavily. Just from the way Rude Boy kept sending his bullets my way, I knew that he intended to kill. I took cover behind my car, and a bundle of slugs penetrated the side, sounding like hail falling from the sky. A couple of my men were retreating slowly, and within a second, two of them were biting the sidewalk from the gang of bullets that riddled them. Nino continued to shoot, but my mind was also on finishing this shit.

Before I could return another shot, he was snatching me into the car and reversing it down the street at full speed.

"What the fuck are you doing?! We let them get her back. Without her, he's gonna go all the way out. We need to handle business." I tried to open the car door and jump out.

"Taki, what the fuck are you doing?!" He snatched me again. "We can't do nothing about this. We need to regroup. You're gonna fucking die and so are the rest of us," he yelled before beating a U-turn and flushing straight for the district line.

"I don't run from anyone. Don't ever do that again. Ever!" I pressed my gun against his head while his focus was on driving.

He cut his eye at me, breathing nervously.

"I'm not telling you how to operate, Taki. I'm not, but you have to be smart and stay alive in order to do what you've planned. I'm on your side," he reasoned calmly.

I slowly released my anger and snatched my gun back. I pulled at my hair, thinking about the fuck up, and I needed a real chess move in order to get my position back to number one. I was willing to do whatever I needed. There were no other choices.

"Call more soldiers. We have a meeting, and I need a team to go and pay a few of his associates a visit. He won't get far around Atlantastan without me knowing what is next. I'm gonna beat him to the punch," I ordered, rubbing my temple in frustration.

"Understood," he agreed and proceeded to handle my request.

Time was on a scale now, and you could bet on my soul that I was going to ensure it leaned toward me in the end.

∽

Private Airport
District 9
Fulton Industrial Boulevard

I THANKED GOD THAT I REUNITED WITH MY WOMAN, AND I was placing a strategy together with every second that passed. After the recent incident with Taki earlier, shit was too dangerous to take any risks with getting Shanti hurt or taken again. Taki had eyes all over the city, and now it was time to move strategically on this lunatic ass bitch. It pained me to see a woman I considered my best friend in this whole world organize my downfall, let alone doing it for my commitment to her like she was a damn mad woman I played or something. A lot of this shit that was going on confused me heavily, but I did realize that Taki had been concealing secret feelings about me for a long time. I always treated her like a queen and spoiled her like she was my own woman, but I never tried to commit to her when we had already been friends for so long. She handled every position I'd given her with my operation faithfully, but she'd fallen in a sick love spell in the same motion.

Stepping out of the car, I ordered JoJo and a few of my soldiers to monitor the area as I handled my business with Shanti. The night air was thick, and the traffic was light. The captain of the plane waited in front of the checking office with his leg kicked up. A cigarette hung from his lips, and his blank expression looked as if he didn't want to be receiving a call in the middle of the night.

"George, I'm glad that you could make it. I hate bothering someone in the middle of resting hours, but it was more than beneficial." I nodded, grabbing ahold of Shanti's hand.

"Likewise. I wouldn't be out for anything else. You know what you're asking me to do can get me a prison sentence. Traveling through the air over no flight territory is hard to do, but you can bet I'm the man for the job."

"That's the reason I called. I have your money." I reached inside the duffle, handing him a manila folder with a hundred grand inside.

"It's much appreciated. If it's okay with you, I'd like to get this show on the road. We're on borrowed time here. I'll start the engine." He shrugged, walking off.

I turned to Shanti, looking her in the eyes, and placed a big kiss on her soft lips.

"I know this is hard for you, but we gotta be thankful and cautious with you being back in our safety. I gotta send you home with your father, only until I finish this shit, ya hear me? I'm gonna be fine, love. It's only for the good."

"Rude, why can't we just leave like we said before, baby? We have money; we have connects. We can say fuck this war zone and start new. Just us. Those weeks were the worst. I thought I was gonna die, and now you're telling me to leave you behind and depend on prayer to bring you home to us. I don't feel good about this." She started to let her tears roll down again.

I knew she had a point, but as long as Taki and Daffy were running out there, we would always have this shit stuck over our heads. I needed to dead this shit and deal with Lo, so I could sleep in peace when I rested my head at night.

"Listen, Shanti, we will do everything we said and more. You know your man ain't going out bad, but this isn't an option. All these people have to go. They took you first so imagine if they had the opportunity to do anything again. It could be all of us. I can't allow that. I won't allow that. Everything is already in place for you at home. You're gonna go through three different ports and planes, and when you reach your destination, your father will be waiting. The quicker I evaporate this issue, the faster I can get back to you all. I love you, and I need you to trust me."

The sound of the plane's engine started, and I could feel the moment coming to a cease. I was relieved to see her away from this, but not away from my protection.

"I love you too, baby. Please be safe." She kissed me once more.

"Just about ready to get in the air, Rude Boy. I don't think we can spare any minute with this long travel." George appeared back around the corner with his arms folded.

"I'll always be safe. You just be waiting for me to get back. Go ahead." I nodded toward the private jet.

She smiled, grabbed her suitcase and duffel, and walked off. George nodded with assurance and escorted her onboard to prepare for her takeoff. Business was business, and Taki, along with Daffy, were about to be held accountable for their actions. My mind was spinning a thousand miles a minute, and I knew I had to move smart with this problem. I didn't want to die in this shitty ass ghost town, so I was prepared to knock down anything in my path.

I stood on the side of the landing lane, watching as the aircraft started to move. It took a minute to roll out on the landing, but as the speed picked up, I watched it reach the end of the runway and lift gently into the air. I spotted Ghost walking up to me out of my peripheral. He was a true savage at his best, and I was more than grateful for the love he'd shown with helping me get Shanti back. Angels came in mad disguises.

"You good over here, my nigga. Trust and believe I know how you feel. I got two that I'm with, and the issues are very similar. I have to apply pressure about them twenty-four seven. Just moving forward though, it's what you're gonna have to cut loose. You'll get yourself killed if you don't." He posted on the wall next to me.

"What do you mean? That's just a feeling I'm always gonna have naturally. I'm definitely focused."

"Right. If I was to open your brain right now, she'll be running all through your shit. I say that with all sincerity when I tell you to cut her from your mind, even your emotions, while she's gone. These emotions will cause you to slip somewhere down the line because it's a weak spot, even if it's everyone else around you that gets the bad end. I had to do the same in order to keep my fam safe, and when it was done, I was able to go back and receive those same feelings and respect. You have blood in the air, and if you're gonna go at these people necks, your mind and heart should be pumping nothing but murder, lil bro. I don't speak this shit; I live it, bruh." he responded smoothly

He stared me directly in the eyes, and I knew that he was serious. In a way, he was right. I didn't like to force my old ways out because, sometimes, I could get out of hand. I honestly didn't have a choice, and this wasn't anything that I could be playing around with. I was going to kill every last one of them until I closed this chapter for good.

"I respect that, and you're right. I'm doing this for the sake of my family, and I appreciate you for riding as far as you have. I'm not gonna drag you along when you got your own blood to tend to."

He looked at me with a smirk and shook his head.

"Nigga, if I didn't wanna be here, I would've been caught flight. I ain't gonna step out on you while this shit is hot. Shit, I wanna kill me a few of these pussies. They shot at me and still didn't get off. I'm just saying though. If you gone end this shit, let's handle business and disperse from this fucking state. I've already got old skeletons around this bitch." He lit up a rolled blunt with a careless expression.

I shook his hand, and we both headed back to our crew that waited at the entrance of the airport strip. Agent Porter was with us every minute of the day now, and I didn't know what position she held now that Shanti was out of harm's way, but I was going to let her coast to confront her business as well. It was only fair, and I was a man of my word. All gloves were off.

∼

Agent Jamiyah Porter
Federal Building, Downtown Atlanta

. . .

It was the following morning after our savage escapade with Mendez when I was called in by my supervisor to the office. Over ten people were left dead in the streets of Atlantastan, and there was a clear message that the authorities were the ones responsible for the actions. I didn't have time to come up with an excuse, neither did I have the care for making up one. After the life of my partner was taken, it placed me in the state of mind to defend his honor by capturing the criminal and walking away from this deceiving piece of shit job that promised to protect and serve.

Making my way to the floor, I walked past a few of my colleagues that had nothing to say but were watching me the entire time I walked to the chief's office. I knew it was about to be a bad day, and I was prepared. When I crossed his threshold, he looked me in the face and shook his head in disapproval.

"Have a seat, Agent Porter."

Sitting down in the chair, I waited quietly as he processed whatever the hell he was about to say.

"Yesterday, I received a call about an all-out war in District 5, not just with one of the most notorious crews in Atlanta but also with the agency that's meant to stop the same catastrophes that you just implemented. Just explain this to me. What in the hell possessed you to go out and get involved with something so stupid? You're literally one of the best agents on this force. I can't say that still sits in my mind the same. There were ten deaths yesterday, and your name is written on some of it." He folded his arms with a heated expression.

"Sir, I don't have any idea what you're talking about. I haven't killed anyone. I was doing a routine search out in District 5, and a couple affiliates from the Kiss Squad began to open fire on me. I defended myself and immediately evacuated the scene because I was alone. I think I walked into the middle of a war at the wrong time. There were two different crews retaliating against each other."

"And let me guess — this other crew would have to be the wolves and savages from District 7. These fucking animals have no hearts or care for morals and life. The same people that we are looking to exterminate the first chance we get. It's kind of awkward that you would be in the same place as Khalifa when this transpired. Is there anything you need to alert me on?" he asked with a suspicious tone.

I held my ground and refused to let his crummy ass fold me because I wanted to do a job that he wouldn't.

"You have the audacity to have any suspicious accusations against me when half of this crooked ass force has sold out for money and God knows what else. My partner is dead because of somebody in District 7, and it's my job to find out by any means necessary. I don't see you making any effort to dig for any information while we all go out and do the footwork of this agency."

"That's because it's not my fucking job to do that, Agent Porter. I am supposed to devise ways to balance this city out before it falls completely to disaster. That means we all lose to the underworld of this fucking warzone. You think that you're the only one who's grieving about losing Lace. The entire force is at odds about it, but we have to take our time with snatching the right person. 2024 experienced the worst war against the people of this city and the government. Hundreds of loyal, dedicated agents and police died for the cause of the bureau. That incident allowed these fucking criminals to take over eighty percent of this city, and we've still had yet to gain a piece of that back."

"I'm fighting daily to make that change, sir, but I just need the opportunity to dig a little further to see. I have an informant at the federal detention center that's helping me wiggle through a few cracks and..."

"Agent Porter, that informant that you're speaking on was murdered in his cell last night by the Mexican Cartel. This wasn't even eight hours after we received the notice about the District 5 incident. The only thing I need you to do is clear your mind of this entire situation. Clear your head with Agent Lace, the agency, and anything else dealing with Khalifa, the Kiss Squad, or this case." He spoke calmly.

"Sir, I understand, but we have a great chance at cracking this entire thing. A little more time is all I need."

Before he could reply, the sound of his office door opening

caused me to turn around. I noticed a well-dressed white man in a black suit enter, and his face wasn't pleasant.

"Good evening, Agent Porter. I'm Agent Wilburn, CIA. I'll be the one taking over this case, and you're free to leave now." He alerted me with a blank face.

"What?! I've been on this case since the beginning. You can't do that. My entire career depends on catching these people for the justice of our agency. Sir, he can't do this!" I stood up to my feet.

My supervisor exhaled, lowering his vision from me.

"Agent Porter, this is the backlash that I warned you about. I told you to let it play by the book, and in due time, all would have prevailed. This incident in District 5 yesterday has forced bigger authority to step in, and I can't help you from that. Porter, you're terminated from the agency indefinitely. Please turn in your gun and badge," he said while looking down at the floor.

My heart nearly fell from my chest when he spoke the command. I tried to register it with no emotion, but the tears instantly began to fall.

"You're firing me?"

"I'm sorry, Porter. It's over my head."

Snatching the badge and gun off my hip, I threw it across his desk forcefully. My entire life had been dedicated to serving the law, and it was spat back with disrespect and corruption. My mission was far from over, even it meant me pursuing the leader of this city on my own.

"Shove it up your ass and you can surely believe that this will not end here. I'll take every crooked individual in this agency down however I have to!" I snapped before storming out his office.

Rushing outside to my car, I immediately began to cry my heart out, but I knew that would get me nowhere. The mission I needed handled was all I had left to avenge Lace's murder, and I would do it with whatever help necessary. I immediately started to form a plan in my head and knew that I had to go and see Rude Boy.

Cranking my engine, I pulled off into traffic, making my way to his new location.

RUDE BOY

District 7

QLS Gardens Apartments

After getting off the phone with Shanti and her father, Mr. Yustafa, I got word that she landed safely in the country and was finally out of harm's way. She was my biggest worry. I never allowed myself to grow with emotions so much with anything in this world, but with her, the feeling was completely different. She gave me life when I exhaled nothing but darkness. I was in perfect harmony with her and the family, and she was just the piece to my puzzle. Taki, on the other end, was a disturbed bitch that I thought was my best friend. She played under my nose with learning everything about me, so she could one day possibly take it all away. So many of my associates were dying from thar reason, and it sickened me to the bottom of my stomach.

"How in the fuck did you let my people die sending him in a separate mission from us? We were supposed to stick together. Since we've been here, shit has fallen. Yazi is dead, and he never wanted to even come back to Atlanta for his Cuban family. Seven is dead because of you!" Dahlia pointed her finger at me sternly.

I couldn't blow on her because I was feeling heavy from these boys losing their lives for the cause of me and my situation. They came to help fight for Shanti, and now, she was safely away, while they were both gone. That shit hurt deeply.

"Dahlia, I never meant for anyone to get killed, but what the hell do you think we're out here doing to these other people we fighting against? Murder doesn't just go one way. It's free for all around this bitch, and this is what comes with it. You can leave if you choose. I'll give you your money, and at least you can walk away with that because just making it out of Atlantastan ain't promised. Karma is nasty, so I accept shit how it comes, and that's just the truth."

"He's right, lil mama. Fuck all that whining you doing, girl. I've been in this game for a long time, and ain't shit beating the double but the triple we gotta push down on these people and try to end this." Ghost waved her off with a nonchalant expression.

"Lo is smart, Rude. He might be impatient when it comes

to making decisions, but he doesn't hesitate to put something better together right after. I hate everything about him. He doesn't care about anyone, only his reputation," JoJo said as he posted against the wall by the window.

"I hear you, lil bro. I know this shit is hard for all of us, but I know the hatred that has been built up against us is finally piling over. Regardless of your relationship with this nigga, I would never force you to go back with him if you really don't want to. You're like my family too, ya know?" I nodded with understanding.

Hearing the knock on the door caused all of us to jump up with our guns in hand.

"Who the fuck is that?" Ghost asked, ready to kill if necessary. "I thought you said nobody knew about this location?"

"Nobody does," I whispered back. "JoJo, answer it." I gave him the green light to handle whatever threat was on the other side.

He glanced out the peephole and huffed before opening the door slowly. When my eyes met Agent Porter's, she had a face full of tears and looked to be lost.

"I need your help." She spoke in a weak tone.

"What the fuck? The cop? I'm not smelling her just knowing our whereabouts like we on a fucking tracker, man." Dahlia lowered her gun with a mug.

Ghost looked at me with a raised eyebrow, but I didn't hesitate to walk over and pull her in before quickly scanning the perimeter outside.

"Agent Porter, what are you doing here? We don't supposed to meet until tomorrow." I looked her up and down.

"I got fired today. I didn't know what else to do. I have nothing else to breathe for besides catching the person that made the lives of so many others a tragedy. I can't do that without you." She quickly gathered her emotions, looking me in the eye.

"Now you need our help? We have our own set agenda. No one gives a fuck about who you desire to lock up and throw away the key." Dahlia jabbed at her again.

Agent Porter closed the distance between them in a flash, and I didn't even have time to grab her.

"Or how about I just beat the fuck out of you and figure out why the hell you're even speaking to me in the first place, you little bitch? I'm talking to him!" she yelled with her fist balled tightly.

"Hey, hold the fuck up. This is what we don't have time for, ya hear me?" I pulled her back by the arm.

Ghost obviously read my mind because he pushed Dahlia toward the kitchen, motioning for JoJo to follow him as well. I could still hear her little crazy ass screaming out reckless shit, just fucking the vibe up even more.

"Listen, you can't just be ready to crash out like that because we have a set mission too. Everything happens at the right time, but right now, she's a part of this team. I understand that you going through a lot as well, but staying calm is the best way to win through it all."

She folded her arms, not trying to hear my speech at all.

"Right, calm. Your girl is off to safety after I helped you get her back. Let alone, the night before having you drop dick in me like I was her has me feeling real calm and confident right now, Rude Boy. I can't say that I didn't know what I was doing because I'm grown, so it's my slip. Now, I've lost my life, what separated me from caring about any of that. I need your help finishing this, so I can take this crooked ass agency down. You owe me that at least." She looked me in the eyes with all sincerity.

I knew that I couldn't deny her because she was more than the reason Shanti was back in my life, but this move was playing real sticky in these streets when it came to not being noticed.

"I will help you by all means, but you have to listen as well. What happened between me and you is normal. It wasn't my intentions on making you feel any type of way. If I did, I apologize, but don't act like you didn't need it or you wasn't feeling mutual with my actions. That's done, and now, I wanna help you, so can we handle business or not?"

"I'll be waiting, but this time, I'm not going anywhere. I hope you have enough room for one more guest," she stated with a look of seriousness.

I exhaled, knowing that I had a load on my hands with this girl. I needed to handle all affairs, so I could catch a flight straight out of this hellhole for good.

Taki

My mind was set on a mission, a plan to kill every stupid person that caused me to lose what I desired. I wasn't a bitch that needed therapy, neither did I need any advice on how I was conducting business around territory that I would eventually have complete control over. I needed understanding. Any source of help that Rude Boy decided to receive assistance from would have to answer to me whether they wanted to or not. I had no certain picks on who would face my wrath for jumping into business that wasn't theirs. It was a part of our tradition. I was just going to show each individual how serious my business was to me.

I set up a meeting with one of the best connections in Atlanta, the man that seemed to get everyone's feet wet when it came to finding their way in our society. He would be my first victim to eliminate and one of the hardest associates to run across face-to-face. Thanks to Daffy, I received that chance a lot sooner than I thought.

He had been in the Cuban restaurant for over ten minutes with a few of my other men, and once I received the text to come in, I strolled in like the biggest queen in the world. I walked with two of my killers toward Kamo and Daffy as they sat at a secluded table by themselves. I spotted the three guards that posted around the alcove as if they were unnoticed. I was already ten steps ahead, and these dudes were past dead before I even made the call.

"Hello, gentlemen. I don't mean to interrupt, but truly, I don't care of course." I sat at the table, grabbing a glass of champagne.

"Uh, am I missing something here, Daffy? This is a private meeting. What is she doing here?" Kamo looked at me with disgust.

"Well, Kamo, I forgot to tell you. She's in position over this operation. It was a slight misunderstanding," Daffy replied.

"Misunderstanding? Where is Rude Boy?" Kamo looked back-and-forth between the two of us.

Without giving any word, my killers stood to their feet and executed the three men that were standing guard. The gunshots that sounded off startled Kamo, forcing him to jump in his chair. His men dropped to the floor, and the civilians sitting around at the tables screamed loudly before stampeding out of the restaurant.

"Daffy, what is the meaning of this? You can't expect this disrespect to stand without retaliation." He fidgeted with nervousness.

I crossed my legs, laughing at his small threat. If only he knew about the chaos I was planning to implement on this town, he would've taken his steps lightly and thought before he mixed his authority into my business.

"Kamo, I'm not sure if you understand my standpoint, so I'll be clear in breaking it down thoroughly for you. Rude Boy is no longer in charge of any district. He's no longer your go-to boy when you feel that you can have things done in my city. You sent assassins to go against the Kiss Squad, and that was probably the biggest mistake that you've ever made in your life. My brother is dead, men from my team have perished because of your stupid actions, and even a man of power like you have to pay for your mistakes, Kamo."

"You sound insane. My people will cut this city upside down and delete every person from this soil if anything ever happens to me."

"I don't know who you think I am, neither do I think that you understand the severity of what I'm telling you. I am this city. I am the dictator, and I am the one who's gonna exterminate everyone Rude Boy has ever rubbed palms with before I kill him. Now, this isn't about money or territory. It's about respect so be mindful that this is just business." I dug in my bag politely.

"I don't care what you think. I…"

His words were cut short from the sharp blade as I leaned across the table and slashed his throat. I watched his head fall to the marble wood, flushing blood all over the white eating covers. I cut my vision at Daffy. He was looking at me with the crazy eye like I had completely lost my mind. The fun in my head was only beginning. The terror hadn't even started yet.

"You killing Kamo is only gonna set off a spark in every district to go against us. He's a friend of the table. You weren't supposed to do that." He stood up from the table with his arms in the air.

"Calm the fuck down. I wouldn't give a fuck if he was the table. Nobody is off limits. I stand on that firmly when I say it. The fate is the same for the rest of them that's on the blacklist." I stood up and strutted toward the door.

"You're gonna create a world of trouble that you're not gonna be able to handle."

"I know. That's why we're gonna handle it," I addressed before leaving my sinister trail in the restaurant.

Rude Boy

It was early in the a.m. when my senses kicked in while I was still in my sleep. The hairs on my arm stood up like a sore thumb, and I immediately reached for the gun beside my pillow.

Leaping out of the bed and moving to the bedroom door, I

cracked it open and noticed JoJo standing in the hallway with his gun in hand as well.

"Did you hear something?" I whispered loud enough for him to hear.

"I think so," he replied, inching farther around the corner.

The next thing witnessed was the silencer of a gun stretch out, but JoJo was quick on his toes. Slapping the gun loose from the hand, I realized it was a white man wearing a mask. The next motion he came with was the knife in his opposite grip, which he jammed straight into JoJo's left arm.

I struggled to aim, not wanting to shoot JoJo, but he pushed him with all his force, causing me to lock in directly on his head.

Boom! Boom!

I let go on the trigger twice, striking him once in the face, and the second bullet hit him the shoulder.

"Aghhh!"

He let out a scream before crumbling to the ground motionless. "JoJo, you good?" I tried to run to his aid.

Once I reached him, I felt the hands of someone as they wrapped me up into a chokehold and crossed their legs around my waist. I could easily tell that it was a woman, but her grip was so tight that it forced me to fall backwards, sending us tumbling down the small staircase. Rolling to the bottom, I quickly rolled away from her grasp to face this bitch head on. It was like she imitated my exact action because she rose just as I did, but her gun was being pulled from her waist. The sight of Ghost appearing behind her in the kitchen caught my sight, and his gun was already aimed.

Boc!

The bullet pierced the back of the assassin's head, draining her immediately. He maneuvered over to me just as JoJo was slowly making his way downstairs with his gun in the opposite hand.

"Uh, I think we got some visitors, but my suggestion would be to get the fuck up outta here while we can before more motherfuckers start jumping through the window." Ghost aimed his gun, scanning the house with his eyes.

"Let's go. Where the fuck is Dahlia?" I asked, still confused from the situation that had just spiraled out of thin air.

"Don't know and we can't give two fucks right about now." Ghost opened the door, stepping out first.

It was either God or this bitch was setting us up because Agent Porter was pulling directly in as we were leaving. When she jumped out of the car, that was when the shots started to ring out again.

Boc! Boc! Boc! Boc! Boc! Bocc! Bocc!

She pulled her gun, ducking for cover, as we all rushed for the cars. Ghost and JoJo jumped inside of my car, and I was closer to Agent Porter's, so I quickly leaped into her front passenger seat. The sparks off the car, alerted me that we were dealing with some professional shooters.

She wasted no time, slamming on the gas, doing a full U-turn and flushing out of the apartments with Ghost directly behind her.

"What the fuck did I just walk into?!" She tried to catch her breath while driving and looking into the rearview mirror.

"You don't think I was trying to figure the same damn thing out, huh?" I checked my gun clip and clamped it back in.

"Well, you're the one with all the plans. I would think you at least knew what was taking place at a location that you only have the whereabouts on," she replied back sarcastically.

I was about to respond, but her statement bounced around my brain like a bullet. She was absolutely right, but now wasn't the time to even throw accusations around in the air. I needed a few hours to put my keys and pieces together, and I was turning the hunt on for Lo, Taki, and the rest of her flunkies full throttle.

"We gotta link everyone together, so we can put this shit to rest. We ain't got no more waiting on our side."

"I have somewhere we can go after you address this and call it for what it is. That'll be the direction I'm pushing in, so you might wanna make this the quickest conversation you can," she stated, looking over at me.

I intended it to be the last time I spoke on what needed to be done until it was handled.

"Just get us there." I watched in the side mirror as Ghost trailed us closely.

AGENT JAMIYAH PORTER

The sun hadn't even settled yet, and we were sitting in District 13, across from this lunatic, Taki's home. The sight of a black Yukon pulling into the driveway was the spark for Ghost and Rude Boy. They didn't hesitate to jump out unnoticed and creep up behind the men who stepped out of the truck. I wanted to stop them to approach it a better way, but I wasn't about to wait around in the car alone. By the time I paced across the street, I watched them both slide up behind the men, striking them both at the same time. Rude Boy followed up with another strike to his victim's head, leaving them both out cold.

"Don't you think we could have waited for them to get in the house before we risked being seen in the streets?" I whispered, looking down at both of the men on the ground.

Rude Boy grabbed one of the men under his arms and

pulled him toward the front door. Ghost followed next, grabbing the second man. Using the keys that were on the ground, we made our way into the home and secured the locks. It was dark and quiet, and I instantly moved to turn on a light.

"No! Don't turn them on. Trust me." Rude Boy grabbed my hand quickly.

Using his flashlight from his cell, Ghost moved around until he found a couple of thick bed sheets in a side closet. Ripping them in lines, he wasted no time tying the men up in restraints.

Rude Boy moved around the home, grabbing certain things and searching with a purpose.

"Do you really think we should be here? It feels awkward sitting in this crazy bitch's home." I asked, being sure to clutch my gun just in case.

"Tell me about it. I'm just looking for anything that can help us know exactly what this bitch is up to. Taki is smart, and I know she is definitely dangerous, but reckless people always have a fall somewhere." I watched him log onto her computer and click on a few different buttons. He focused on reading whatever was in front of him while I witnessed the two men on the floor starting to come back to consciousness.

"The stooges are awakening." I took a step back, ready to pop one of their asses if necessary

Rude Boy sat quietly on the computer for a second longer before closing it slowly. Standing to his feet, he proceeded back over to where Ghost stood over them both.

"I'm glad you pussy holes could wake and face me like a man. Of course you know that if I'm here, it's business that we need to address." Rude spoke harshly.

The men tried to speak at once, but their words only jumbled over one another's.

"Both of you shut the fuck up. You disloyal snakes are only good for lying, so the excuses are only more seconds deducted from me bussing you fuck boys' head. I wanna know what Taki is plotting. Who else is she associating with to pull something so stupid?"

"You know these guys?" I asked, confused.

"Yeah, Nino and Joker. They were workers for me at a point of time, but this bitch rewired these idiots' brain somehow."

"Rude, Taki is gonna kill you. Betrayal should be the last thing on your mind dealing with us. Why the fuck do you think we disappeared? We couldn't stop this bitch if we wanted to, so you think we're gonna risk our lives for a woman that is obsessed with you? She's working with every district in this city to see you and that girl bleed. She's taking every risk to ensure it happens, stupid!" Nino looked up at me as he spoke.

"Man, fuck that. The bitch has 2.5 mill behind the fridge. We were on our way to steal the shit and get the fuck outta here. Free me and you can keep that shit, and I'll still leave," Joker added nervously.

Rude Boy looked at them angrily, bending down.

"Where is Daffy?"

One acted as if he wasn't going to spill it, but the Joker character didn't waste any opportunity.

"That nigga ass is in District 11 in the suburbs. It ain't just easy getting through them streets with all the Kiss Squad niggas that be snooping around that area."

"That shouldn't be a problem." I raised my gun, placing two slugs into both of them.

Boc! Boc! Boc! Boc!

Silence filled the air, and he wasted no time heading for the refrigerator, sliding it off from the wall. Me and Ghost followed and slightly watched over his shoulder. There was a small, plastered wall behind it, and he smashed it completely in with the handle of his gun. The large bundles of cash that started to fall from behind it made him pause before he quickly grabbed a bag and started to fill it up. Tossing the first one to Ghost, he continued to fill another before standing up.

"Let's go." He nodded toward the door.

Making our way out, we moved smoothly to the car before climbing back inside. The cash that was in the bags they carried was the most I'd seen in my entire life. The clashing that was coming behind these crazy ass people's actions were getting beyond personal, and something told me that I was going to end up deeper into this pit than I thought. My heart could feel it.

Taki

"That's what I'm talkinggg bout! Get in that pussy," I moaned, feeling myself come to ecstasy on top of Daffy's dick.

He continued stroking me smoothly as I bounced the hormones out of my system for the second time. Daffy's shit was more than good, but it was only used to picture Rude Boy's cock in me to have a baby. His games were minor to me at first because of our friendship and how much I deeply loved this nigga, but falling in my arms and climbing inside of me when he was mad at Shanti only angered me when he would act as if nothing had even happened the days after. The audacity had me more than pissed, and now that I knew my feelings were on a back burner, I was going to place everyone he loved inside of a pot that was scorched by my hands personally.

"Damn, you feeling good, huh?" Daffy asked me as I climbed off top of him and headed for the bathroom.

"Nothing special," I uttered before making my way inside. I quickly showered and put on my apparel — a long, silk, Chanel dress that came down to my ankles and a pair of black, strappy Christian Louboutin heels. After applying my makeup, I gathered my bag and two 9mm handguns. Looking at Daffy get dressed, I paused.

"I hope you know to stick with the plan I informed. Five of the squad members is coming with me, so there's three left on security. Send soldiers out to sniff out Rude Boy and this mystery slut he's running with. I don't care what they have to do. Find out who she is," I demanded.

"I'm on that shit already. I told you I'm not playing. Long as you listen to me as well, I got you," he assured with a nod.

Leaving without a reply, I made my way to the parking lot where two cars of my men waited for me. The backdoor of my vehicle was opened when I approached it, and I climbed inside, closing the door myself.

"District 1," I informed my young hitter that was driving.

I was bolder than most thought, and Rude Boy fucked with the wrong feelings. He had to pay, either with his eternal commitment to me or death just like the rest of his pawns already had coming.

It took me over thirty minutes to make my way downtown. When I arrived at the building, I stepped out with four of my men on my trail. I entered the Loft Complex and took the elevator up to the top floor. When we steeped off, six guards immediately approached us and tried to frisk us down.

"Don't worry. We all have guns. Unfortunately, they go everywhere we do. Tell Lo I'm here to see him." I stared at them fiercely.

One of the guards moved inside his Loft suite and returned a few moments later, whispering into another guard's ear. They all stepped to the side and allowed us to enter. I strolled inside his residence as if I owned it, and all my men waited at the door as I approached him, taking a seat at his table.

"Well, I'm glad that you decided to make it. I can't say that it's a pleasure knowing how evil you are, but it is a pleasure seeing your appearance as always." He sat back in his chair with a cigar between his fingers. The table was filled with delicious fruit and beverages, and I didn't hesitate to help myself to a glass of his Ace of Spades champagne that was hugging the table.

"It's never a pleasure seeing you, Lo, and I only know that because I've worked for you. It's business, and the last time I checked, you called me for business. I have some killing to do, so I'm kind of on a time schedule. What the fuck do you want?" I spat before filling another glass.

He shook his head before clearing his throat.

"I see that you've taken it upon yourself to start an all-out war with District 7. Rude Boy was once a loving associate, and now you're chasing down his life for a reason that I'm clearly not understanding."

"It's not your fucking business to understand it. It's personal, and my reign will not end until I win."

"Taki, you do know that it's rules to going at any district in this city. Your past few incidents in these recent days has been in violation of numerous district leaders' territory. Lives have been taken unlawfully, and your outrage is being complained about as we speak. Codes were placed in effect."

"I don't give a fuck about any codes or any laws, Lo. How about I explain something to you, slow ass white boy? My crew tarnished this city with the murder rate. The Kiss Squad is why soft ass men like you get to boss shit around like you pulling fucking triggers and making millions. Killing is so simple, but I'm the only brain that can get it implemented in a heartbeat. You see I run majority of this city. I have murderers flooding around this city by the numbers, and I'm always steps ahead. I'm everywhere you think I'm not, and I have the voice to make these renegades light these streets up like Independence Day. You don't run me or my men. Neither will you stop us from doing anything we have on the agenda. I'll disintegrate each district one by one if you think that I'm bluffing," I explained as humbly as possible.

His eyes said that he wanted to reply back with some balls, but my energy was definitely being felt by the load.

"Listen, Taki, you have your operation, and I respect your standing, but remember that I come correctly as well, but my meeting with you today wasn't for that type of connection. Rude Boy has obligations with me as well, and my brother is still in cahoots with this monkey, which is harming my business. I don't care how many die because I have seen many, but I need my relative back in my security. He's more of a priority, and the way your crew is coming right now, he'll end up dead from your hands, and I don't want that type of confliction with you. So, a proposal from my table has been placed up. If you can gain my brother and escort him safely back to me, I allow you to run fifty percent of the city with your own rulings, eight million dollars cash, and a split on all finances you gain from the new districts." He threw the deal of a lifetime on the table.

I smiled, crossing my legs, knowing I had him exactly where I wanted.

"Fifty percent sounds good, and we'll also be sure to handle our part of the deal. Nine million dollars sounds so much better, and splitting profits with you from the new districts is pushing it. I give you thirty percent of all narcotics and merchandise sold throughout the month, but all the business income is profit for my team and their families." I held out my hand, slightly renegotiating the terms.

He exhaled a cloud of smoke, glaring at me with a nasty hatred.

"Every term will remain under my control, and you will not initiate conflict without my awareness." He held his hand out, shaking mine.

"I love when things can be so understood." I smiled, standing to my feet. "Don't you worry your thin, little blonde head. I'll shape shift this problem for you easily."

Walking toward the door, me and my squad members exited his property and were ready to cause some more grief. I was only connecting my dots because his authority was thrown out the window without him even realizing it. Now that my card was green to run this town wildly, I was going to stain the pavement with my name.

Agent Jamiyah Porter

We had just left the district on the west, making alliances with a few more of Rude Boy's associates. The west district held some of the most dangerous killers and also the most sufficient hustlers when it came down to raising the economy for the territory. It was loaded with tons of apartment complexes that housed Muslims and every gang that you could think of if it was allowed in the region. They killed for one another, and the meaning of trenches was beneath their name tag.

"I'm not understanding why you just can't hunt this guy down first and save Taki for last," I suggested, feeling uncomfortable in so many cold-hearted presences. With the number of people involved in this affair, it looked as if it would be an all-out catastrophe for whomever picked the wrong side.

"Lots of these men you see in these different districts hold a certain oath to Lo in some degree. Me aiming for him without alerting the outside sources makes it seem that I'm rising against the leadership. Explaining to them the respect and codes that he broke makes it known I'm not doing it for greed nor money. It's for honor. Some will join beside me, and some won't. It comes with it."

"So, what's next?" I looked over at him.

"Lo has a meeting tonight at a high-end club in District 1. Taki might be there. We're gonna shoot that bitch down and try to catch 'em both. It's dangerous, but it's no room for passing up these chances. This is the way you get your lucky person, and I X mines out as well."

"Sounds fun," Ghost calmly added in from the backseat.

"If it's the shot to put this in the grave, I don't give a damn."

I thought to myself for most of the car ride, and by the time we made our way out to District 7, Rude Boy asked me to pull inside of the Chase bank parking lot.

"What are we doing here?" I asked.

"I'm going in here to stash this money in separate safe deposit boxes. We each will have a key to our own, and two hundred grand will be there in case shit get ugly and we need to bail. It's no telling what might happen, so if shit gets nasty, you can grab the money and have some to get around with."

"I don't need any dirty money. This is only business that I swore by my life I would handle. When it's done, I'm out." I turned my head, gazing out the window.

"I don't give a damn if you take it or not. It'll be there, and it's for you. We only get one chance to make it away free, so if it's needed, take it. Besides that, I don't give a damn." He stepped out of the car with Ghost following him.

They carried two loads of money inside, and I rose out of my driver's seat to catch some air. I didn't know where the hell my life had ended up at, but I was just truly starting to accept whatever the future held. I knew these streets like the back of my hand, so catching every enemy I had wasn't an issue.

"Ms. Porter?" I heard a voice speak out, grabbing my attention.

Looking across from me, Agent Wilburn was dressed in an all-black, Tom Ford, two-piece suit with a pair of dark Ray-Ban glasses. He was staring at me like he had lost something, and my mind immediately went to how the fuck he ended up in my same location.

"Are you fucking following me?" I snapped.

"Of course not. I was actually just coming out to the district to do a little digging on my own. Never expected to actually run into you out and about around this area. Came to visit the bank, I see." He nodded his head toward the building.

I knew that I had to think quick. Rude Boy and Ghost were bound to come out at any minute, and I didn't need this fucking snooping snitch to view me with them for any reason. I was devising a plan in my head when he removed his glasses and stared at me.

"It's something very weird about you, Ms. Porter, and I'm gonna find out, and if it's something that I don't like, you're gonna regret becoming a field agent for the rest of your life. That's a promise," he stated before climbing into his car and pulling off slowly.

I flicked his pussy ass a middle finger, letting him know that I didn't give a fuck, and there was nothing he, or anybody else for that matter, could do to change my mind on what I was trying to handle.

Ghost and Rude Boy appeared out of the building two minutes later, strolling back to the car. Once they climbed in, I started the car and made sure to check my surroundings.

"Don't panic but a CIA agent named Wilburn just confronted me standing in front of the bank. I'm not sure, but it may be some eyes on me after being fired a few days back. The chief may think I'm setting them up or holding back information that could potentially be dangerous to the force."

"Where the fuck did he go?" Ghost pulled his gun, rotating his head anxiously.

"He's gone. He said he's watching me and jumped back in his car to leave. I was just being sure he didn't get a visual on you guys before y'all came out."

"Do you know anything about this dude?" Rude Boy questioned.

"I know a little. I know he's a pain in the ass, and he's definitely snooping around our department, looking for something. I just don't think it's nothing good," I replied before jumping on the expressway, heading back to my home.

"Do you think this guy is gonna be a problem?" he asked with a little worry.

"I don't know."

"Well, we're not slowing down now. We need to stick and move as we go and clean this shit up quickly. I hired a few more dirty men that like to handle business, so it's all or nothing. We ain't stopping until they can't make another movement," he stressed before picking up his cell phone.

I thought about all of the shit that was about to play out, and this was the top of the line. Either our plan would go as it should or we were all about to decorate our own funerals.

RUDE BOY

Club Cheetah
District 1

We had been staking out the club for at least two hours and had yet to make the perfect move without causing too much of a scene. Two Kiss Squad members were armed, standing directly in front of the doors, and one uniformed officer was a few feet away from them, directing guests out of the parking lot. There was a crowd of people still inside, and it didn't look as if it was dying down any time soon.

"Fuck this. Let's go!" I grabbed my gun, climbing out of the car. Ghost and Agent Porter followed as I crossed the street, closing the distance on the security for the spot. As I glanced at Ghost, he smiled before jamming a blade into one of the men's necks and pulled his silenced pistol, knocking a chunk out the center of the second man's head with one shot.

Pwet!

The officer in front of me turned to look, and he never felt me wrap my muscular arms around his neck, twisting in one fast motion. He dropped to the concrete without making a sound, and the only people that were getting out of dodge were the civilians that caught the slight action.

"I need you to stand guard at the door. If anyone on the team show up in your visual, kill they ass dead." I looked at Agent Porter seriously.

Walking through the glass doors first, I raised both of my guns, and Ghost guarded my back. The dim lights were still in use, and the small crowds of people started to get wide eyed from the sight of us stepping on the dance floor. I roamed my eyes swiftly, lurking on our opposition. At the next moment, I turned my head to look at the DJ's booth. I witnessed Lo standing in the glass window, looking down at us calmly. I didn't even hesitate to make my next move.

Raising my guns, I aimed at the booth and released shot after shot.

Boom! Boom! Boom! Boom! Boom! Boom!

The glass shattered as he rushed to move out of the way, and I pushed to make our way through the stampede of left-over guests screaming and trying to make it to the front entrance.

The sound of a bullet flying past my ear forced me to duck low, and I noticed two Kiss Squad members aiming in our direction. The second bullet nearly knocked me on my ass as I went to move. Aiming on one knee, I locked in, and I pulled my trigger twice, catching one of the rookies in the chest.

Boom! Boom!

I didn't stop moving when I saw the nigga's body drop. I heard a few more shots zip through the air, and by the time I zoomed my radar in on the second shooter, Ghost was rising up on the opposite side of his sight.

Boc!

He sent his brains flying over the speakers and wall post.

The club was thinning out, and I quickly made my way back to Ghost's side. Reaching the side stairs that led to the booth, we rushed toward it and were pushed back by a gang of bullets letting loose.

Pak! Pak! Pak! Pak! Pak! Pak! Pak! Pakkk!

Somebody was toting some bigger shit, and we didn't have a choice but to take cover behind whatever we could. Glass and debris were flying through the air from the reckless bullets, but I knew we weren't about to die in this bitch. As I lifted up from behind the sitting booth, I witnessed Lo and Taki heading toward a hallway a few feet from us. I raised my gun to shoot and watched Taki send multiple slugs directly at me.

Boc! Boc! Boc! Boc!

"Shittt! They getting the fuck away!" I yelled over to Ghost.

The lunatic gunman was spraying anything he could, and this pussy, Lo, couldn't believe his eyes when he saw me here. I was too close. Taking a deep breath, I listened as the gun continued to sound off. I exhaled calmly, rose up slightly, and fired three times.

Boc! Boc! Boc!

I wasn't accurate on the first two, but my third found home in my target's neck. The loud clamor deceased, and the empty club was barely standing from the small battle that had just taken place.

"Damn!" I rushed for the hallway they exited through to see if I could get an eye on either of them. I spotted a few doors and moved cautiously, stepping past them. Pushing my way through the back exit door, the parking lot was empty, and I could see the headlights from their car at the far end of the street.

"Shittt! Shitt!" I scrubbed the barrel of the gun across my head in frustration.

It was already bad enough that Lo saw me with his own eyes. Now, the surprise attack wasn't so much of one anymore. I could even see the shock on Taki's face. It forced her to try and take me out from fear that I could have just slain both of them at that exact moment.

"No luck?" Ghost asked as I jogged back through to the dance floor.

"Nah, they gone, but I can guarantee they'll be trying to locate us later. We need to get this team and step now because if we don't, they will," I addressed before we rushed for the doors. Agent Porter held her gun in hand as we exited the building, and a few small crowds watched us as we moved hastily through the driveway of the establishment.

The approaching sound of speeding trucks immediately pierced my eardrums as we were pacing across the street, and within seconds, we witnessed at least six unmarked SUVs surrounding the intersections like a stop light.

We rushed to the car and reached it before the red and blue lights sounded off loudly. As I maneuvered around the car to get in the driver's seat, Agent Porter's eyes grew wide in fear, and she didn't hesitate to raise her gun.

"Rude, get down!" she screamed before I ducked and slid into my car.

Her pistol let off one shot, and my head rotated to see what the fuck spooked her to throw me off track. There was the sight of a man holding his chest and stumbling out the small breezeway, dropping his gun to the ground.

"Get in! Let's go!" I nearly snatched her in before slamming down on the gas pedal. In my peripheral, I watched the Feds crawl out of the trucks like mice, and we only got a few feet in distance before the clinking of their bullets started to tap down on our car. We all ducked from instinct, and I turned the first corner, driving us swiftly through the traffic of downtown.

"Who the fuck was that?" I shot my eyes over to her, confused.

"Fuck! Fuck! Fuck!" she screamed in anger.

"Jamiyah, who was it? Communication is needed right now." I swerved throughout the moving cars, trying to put some space in between us and the small graveyard we'd just created. Not to mention, Lo and Taki were sure to come with all they had. The entire Atlantastan could be hunting for us by morning, and I had no plans of resting easy until both of them were dead.

"That was the agent I spoke to you about earlier," she uttered.

"Who?" I needed to hear her clearly.

"The fucking agent that stopped me at the bank earlier — Wilburn. He was about to shoot you, and I killed him. I'm going all the way under the fucking ground for this one. Damn it!" She covered her face.

I didn't know exactly what to say because I was more than grateful she'd pulled it, or I would've been dead. The thought of murdering her own kind was the principal eating at her, and once a member of law enforcement was killed, you would never fit the image of innocent again.

"Stay calm, ya hear me? We don't leave nobody in the

rain. You saved my life." I gazed at her, wondering why she'd just taken that risk for me.

"We need to grab what we can and relocate immediately. We're looking at a small window, and if we're gonna exterminate this pest problem, we've got some serious mountains about to tumble down on our heads." She took a deep breath as I continued to cruise out of District 1 with murder deep on my mind.

∾

Lo

"I NEED SOMEONE — I MEAN, ANY-FUCKING-BODY — TO TELL me what the fuck was that!" I yelled with my eyes closed, not caring to even look at the so-called team in front of me. "My club is destroyed, and I was nearly killed. When did citizens of this city start to feel that they can attempt death missions against me? I want these filthy bottom feeders to die, and I mean like pronto." I looked around the room at my business associates.

"Lo, you know I've never been the one to give the bad news, but this wasn't a sweet treat. They killed two of my best and believe me when I say it wasn't easy. This vendetta or whatever you all have transpired upon with this clashing, it's getting deeper, and I ain't budging until I know his entire organization is sleep." Di'meech spoke with a low but sinister tone.

"I'll tell you just like anybody that decides to ask. This shit comes with it. I would like to know how the fuck they knew about us meeting at the Cheetah in the first place. They made the stupid attempt, and now, it's gonna cost them dearly. They can't run. We can reach to whatever limits. They ignited a fire, and I'm gonna blaze it up a little more," Taki ranted with arrogance.

I hated her guts most of the time, but when it came to prioritizing steps to win, she was a rabbit foot. This was a side I'd never seen before. JoJo was the piece to this headache ending, and Rude Boy had just made it ten times worse.

"Place out a memo. I have five million for whoever brings me his headfirst and wipes out his entire district. If they can succeed with retrieving my brother, I'll pay another five with interest. What do you all need, killers? I'll pay for 'em. Whatever the hell it takes." I opened the bottle of whiskey and took a good sip of it.

"I have Daffy on speed dial, and we're already on point with new men. This is a game of chess, and something tells me they're gonna fall right into our hands. You need to call the scary guy in your back pocket and tell him we need some info on someone," Taki proposed.

"Who?"

"This bitch." She turned her phone around, showing me the picture of the woman.

I had never seen her before, but I didn't see her having any valid reason to play with the reaper for the sake of Rude Boy. Using my cell phone, I screenshotted her photo and dialed a number in my keypad.

"I don't know, but it shouldn't be hard to find out."

AGENT JAMIYAH PORTER

Arriving at my home, we gathered all the necessary gear we needed, and I rushed to snatch my passport and a little personal information for times like these. Jumping into a pit of blood with this guy, Lo, was suicidal. It was a duty to me on finding the head corruption in Atlanta to kill the cycle. A great man that I called a fiend died, forcing me to work even harder for the takedown.

We moved around, loading guns, and I used the extra four Kevlar vests that were stashed in my basement to ensure us all a little extra protection. My eyes happened to gaze up at the flat screen that was mounted on my wall. The state news was live on air, and I couldn't even be surprised when I noticed my picture on the righthand side of the storyline.

"Well, I be damn. That was quick." Ghost shook his head while adjusting his gun.

I looked over at Rude Boy with a torn facial expression, and it was nothing but havoc to come now that the law would be pursuing me instead. I was destroyed on the inside for how my good turned wrong, but I was prepared for what was next because I would never lay down for doing what was right.

"Try not to even worry about that. You can't allow it to drag you, or you're gonna lose in the end. You can't change nothing, but we can try and direct it to have the best outcome possible." He tried to comfort me.

"It doesn't matter anymore. We need to get the fuck outta here and hunt these people down before they get away with all this shit they created. I'm disappearing after this, and the entire law enforcement of the United States can kiss my ass."

Feeling my cell phone vibrate, I pulled it from my pocket. It was my superior, and it was guarantee that he wasn't about to have anything pleasurable to say. I answered, still wanting to clear the air on my case and allow for my fate to take place.

"Hello?"

"You've screwed up big time, Porter. You're fucking done. I warned you, but you had to test the waters with my orders, huh?" His anger was pumping through the receiver.

"I'm only doing a job that I was paid to do. Fighting for our cause and snatching the justice back from the oppressors was the objective, sir. You and this department aren't fighting for nothing but survival, and I stood for what was right. I didn't mean for Wilburn to be a victim in any manner, but this matter has gotten out of hand. Someone has to end it," I replied.

"You aren't about to end anything but your freedom when you finally get thrown inside of a tomb for eternity. You are not an active FBI agent with this force, and you have no authority to do anything proceeding with these individuals or the law. Now I don't know if you've been under the influence of drugs or what, Porter, but you need to turn yourself in like right now. Leave me some room to help you. It's only gonna get outrageous from here." He warned me.

Ghost and Rude Boy stared at me as I pondered on what he was telling me. I had gone so far in the mud that if I turned back, there would be no honor with the same results. I couldn't do that.

"I'm not turning myself in. I stand where I should, and I'm not going to stop until I complete my end."

You're gonna get yourself killed, and I can ensure you the force is gonna do the honors with that," he threatened.

"Good luck." I ended the call, tucking away my phone. "I think now is the time to disperse. We have about a seventy-two-hour window to end this shit, or all of us will be dead or in a cage," I warned, grabbing a few more things.

"Whatever it takes. I got a few friends out in the west district that has a place for us to lay low. No one will be able to pinpoint us around these individuals. It's hard to trust anyone right about now." Rude's phone began to ring after he made the statement.

I watched him answer and listen closely to whoever was on the other side of the line.

"Okay, send it to me now." He spoke before hanging up the call.

"What's next?" I asked, looking at him curiously.

"JoJo found this nigga address."

"Who?"

"Daffy."

"So, what are we doing?"

"We're going straight over there. I'll explain the rest as we drive." He tossed his carrying bag across his shoulders, heading for the door.

It was time to extinguish this fire, and more people had to be removed in order to accomplish it. I was prepared to assist with every twist and turn until there was nothing to cause me worry. I killed the lights in my home, knowing it may be the last time I stepped foot inside it.

∽

Daffy

I sat in the crib, pissed at the failed attempt on Lo's life earlier at the club. I didn't intend for Taki to be in the mix of harm's way, but it would have been my calling card to see Lo perish and easily be removed out of my way. His enforcement was a cripple in my plans on taking this shit over. My plan was to swap a few things up when a had the chance, and nothing would be off limits to how I wanted this shit to run.

I had just gotten off the phone with Taki and didn't hesitate to call up a few Kiss Squad recruiters to ensure we weren't lacking. Two of my men occupied the house with me, and my brain was focused on counting the money that had just been made until this situation appeared . This lifestyle was crazy. The houses we resided in were immaculate. Nothing was a cheap expense. I was able to purchase the best designer clothes, ate the best food that cash could buy, and flex my muscle as hard as I needed to show the people who really held the turf down.

"Aye, yo, both of y'all get ready to go and meet these niggas to come out this way. Taki should be back in a few hours, and she wants anybody who's standing with us to be present. Keep your mouths closed about everything, and if it's meant for these clowns to know, she'll be the one that informs them. Handle that and come straight back," I instructed them as I placed on my Cartier watch.

They nodded with understanding and prepared to leave, and my thoughts went to the new young hoe I met that was helping me out a ton with her free insight. It was all a part of the plan, and in due time, shit was going to progress.

As one of my men opened the door, I heard the first gunshot that caused me to jump.

Boom!

I witnessed the back of his head open up like a can before my second guard fell to the floor and started to return fire.

Boc! Boc! Boc! Boc! Boc!

I dashed into the kitchen, rushing for the counter drawer. Reaching inside, I pulled out the Ruger P89 handgun, and the entire house grew black from the power being shut off. I heard one more gunshot release but still had yet to hear any voice. I tried to adjust my eyes to the darkness, blinking repeatedly with my gun still aimed. A line of sweat formed against my eyebrow, and my adrenaline started to kick in.

"I don't know who the fuck came to my shit unannounced, but you're leaving out in a body bag!" I yelled, trying to alert my intruder that I was willing to go all the way out. I took about two steps and felt someone rush me with force, nearly sending me to the floor. My gun dropped to the ground, but I held on to my attacker's arm until my back rammed against the refrigerator. At that exact second, the lights came back to life, and Rude Boy was standing a few feet away from me with his gun aimed to kill. Another man, that hung in the background, stood by the entrance of the kitchen silently. It was as if he was there to watch.

"Nigga, you ain't gone pull it when you know we gonna take everything you loved. You don't scare me, Rude Boy. Always been so smart. You got all this way and didn't die, so you could prove what? You mad cause I stepped away and got money because ya problem is with Taki and Lo, not me. Put the gun down, pussy," I taunted him with a pathetic face as if he was just a hater.

He looked at me with malice in his eyes and didn't hesitate to toss the gun to his accomplice. I smirked in shock, but I knew that he was tougher than he seemed. This was my chance to make a way out, and I was definitely going to take advantage.

"Boy, I'm about to break your whole face." I threw up my guard and stepped toward him.

He wasted no time closing the distance, and once I entered his personal space, we immediately started to trade blows. We fought toe to toe for a good second before he nearly stumbled over his foot. I shot a right hook, catching him in the jaw.

"Yeah, bitch, let's go!" I let him get his balance, so I wouldn't rush it.

I shot a right uppercut, and he dodged it quickly, hitting me in my face three sharp times.

"Fuck!"

I shook it off, feeling my eyes water, and still swung with all my power to try and end the entire ordeal. He took a stiff punch from me but slid closer instead of farther away. I saw his fist coming before I could move, and it crashed directly into my nose. I was dazed from the hit but tried to zone back in. He placed punches, sending me to the floor, and the next thing I felt was his foot colliding with my face.

Rolling onto my back, I tried to catch my breath and breathe from the slight blood that I was choking on.

"You think this makes you win, Rude Boy, huh?" I spoke with a small slur. "I'm just a piece to this shit that will never end, fool. You'll be killing me for nothing."

"The point of me getting rid of you is not personal, stupid boy. You're a snake. A traitor for the materialistic. I trusted you and allowed harm to enter my safe zone because of you. You played it harsh, but I have tricks too, Daffy. Unfortunately, you're not gonna have to worry about any of the next ones." He grabbed his gun from the quiet killer in the corner.

He walked over to me, staring down, before pointing it directly at my face.

"Show me, Rude Boy. Let's see if you can stand on business." I begged him to pull it.

"Always had and always will."

TAKI

Death had taken its toll on my end of the table, and my team was taking major Ls repeatedly as the past few weeks had flown by. I was standing inside Daffy's living room, wondering how this idiot allowed someone to come into his own territory and didn't take anyone with him. Seven of my Kiss Squad soldiers stood around as I vented in the air. It wasn't because Daffy's worthless life was gone and not because I was losing money in the process. It was because of the audacity of Rude Boy feeling as if I wouldn't make his ass bow. I was in need of his respect and let us not forget his sperm to have a piece of that bloodline for myself. After he donated his child to me, he could perish just like the rest of them.

My new recruit, Dahlia, stepped though the threshold, and I immediately waved her over to me.

"Please tell me you have something for me?"

"I've been trying to keep the best eyes on these people since I've started, and they haven't remained in one spot yet. Constant war will make it harder for both sides if no one shows any patience or rational movements. This will keep going until we're all gone." She folded her arms with an expression as if she ran some shit.

"Listen, redhead, you're a pretty girl, and I'm not sure how they run things in California, but we respect authority. Okay, sweetie?" I looked at her through slanted eyes, hoping she replied recklessly.

"Oh, I understand clearly. Just remember that my boss that I came from California with is dead. I'm standing here in this spot because of Daffy, and he laying in the center of the kitchen. Now this guy, Rude Boy, isn't just running alone with his own conscience. There's a fucking FBI agent hounding around him as if she was his sister. Maybe they're fucking. I don't know. From what I know, they want Lo more than anything. All I'm saying is you might need to place a little pause on things, so you can catch this guy exactly where you need him."

I wanted to slit her throat so badly, but she kind of had a point. Patience was a key that a lot of people didn't possess, and I happened to be one of them. Lo would have to catch the attention of these headaches until I could catch Rude Boy at the most vulnerable time. His face was on the borderline of every district, and now that I knew I was dealing with the FBI as well, I guessed I would war it out with the police as well.

"Glad you gave me that little piece of info right there. So, we inform the entire world that he's running with a fucking pig, and no district will trust him. The art of chess is definitely a beautiful game. I'm gonna make you a very rich woman if you can remain loyal and by my side with this venture. Trust that it will be more than exciting."

Rude Boy
Westside District

I ARRIVED OVER IN THE WESTSIDE DISTRICT, AND THE TIME was starting to grow early. It was new rules in our turf, and that was all for one and one for all. This was the side where you didn't have to worry unless you were moving about on some dictator shit. It was banned from the district leader, a leader that just happened to be a friend of mine, Abdullah Zahir. He was an older Muslim that could go head on with anyone in this city. It wasn't the fact of him losing nor how many Muslims or gang affiliates died for the cause. They continued to regroup and come back stronger each time. He was a killer from way back when the Westend Assassins defended the neighborhoods with honor. Now, this new age purge shit had him lifting back up his guards like the Black Panthers were reinvented

I pulled into his large mansion that sat directly at the intersection of Tiger Flowers and Westlake. Not only did he have the biggest crib on the block, but he enforced it all with peace and prosperity. If you were a dealer, respect the non-users and keep it to a minimum. If you were thinking about being a killer, you had to find a new district to relocate, or you wouldn't live another day to harm your next victim.

Me, Ghost, and Agent Porter stepped out of the car, and we were met by Abdullah and a number of his armed henchman.

"Rude Boy, my brudda. It's alhamdulillah to see ya, man. I hate that you didn't come to me earlier." He looked at Ghost, giving a small salute, but when his eyes landed on Agent Porter, his smile turned into a large frown.

"Who is she?"

"She a helper of my team. You know I wouldn't bring any harm to this side period, Abdullah. She's on the same mission we are — to overrule Lo and make this a normal city again." I advocated for her.

"She's a Fed, Rude Boy. Her face is all over the news, my brother. Are you aware of this?" He glanced between me and Ghost.

"Yeah, I'm quite sure that everyone knows. It's nothing to panic about because, surely indeed, it's clear what side I'm choosing. I don't think no individual here wants to see this town flip around more than me, and I can promise you I'll bet my life on it. I don't need any of your help. This was a mistake!" she snapped her head at me and was about to walk off.

I immediately snatched her arm with a disapproving expression before looking back to Abdullah.

"I said she's with me, big bro. She's been down the entire time, and I definitely could have been dead a few hours ago if she wouldn't have shot first before asking questions. Trust me." I nodded with assurance.

He looked at Agent Porter with a gaze that I couldn't explain but accepted my invitation because of my word.

"It's all in your court, my boy. The residence is yours, and it's one of many more I have. This place is more secured than District 1, so I would like it to stay like that. The police creep through on late nights, and they target ones that get closer out of our territory . Stay low and enjoy yourself, man. You know that my safety is your safety." He pointed toward the home behind him.

"You know I owe you for this." I shook his hand and proceeded inside.

This crib was marvelous, and it didn't have the feel of the reckless city we lived upon. We were based of bloodshed and separation when the rules back in the day consisted of more zones and people representing their side. It was just Atlanta. His pad was laced. A touchscreen television occupied every wall in the house, even the kitchen. I could see that he was big on flowers and plants because each room held a vase with a bundle of exotic plants. Surely everything in this bitch was beyond expensive, and even though it felt good, I still knew that my game plan had to be quick and lethal. Lo wouldn't forgive what transpired, so I knew the heat was on. I just prayed that it didn't cause Abdullah any hardship for carrying my extra baggage.

"I could get used to this for a few days." Ghost smirked before tossing his bag on the floor.

"I know that's right." I looked around, still amazed at the decor of this home.

"So, what am I supposed to do, just pick any room? I need to shower," Agent Porter voiced with agitation.

"Sure, it doesn't matter. Abdullah will let us rest as long as we need, but my plan can't be to just lay down right now with all that's on the line. I got a family to get home too."

She didn't reply, but the sadness in her face told me everything. She felt lost after this flipside of her position, and in the end, she felt that she would be left alone. Regardless, I could only extend my help so far before I fell myself, and I couldn't risk me or my foundation for this bullshit. I would leave this bitch for good.

"That girl is slick in love with you, my guy. Shit's all over her fucking face," Ghost mumbled when she walked out of the room.

"I kinda sensed that too. I don't know what the hell is going on anymore, man."

"Nigga, yes the hell you do. Did you fuck her?" He caught me off guard with the question.

I stumbled to answer, and he immediately chuckled, shaking his head.

"Yeah, you did. You started a game that you shouldn't have played, period. The girl risked it all for you in just a few weeks, and trust me, I know the outcome of these situations. One of my wives came from the same field. Now, she's one of the biggest international criminals around the United States. So, trust me, her journey with you is far from over. If it is in your head, you might as well go and shoot that bitch through her skull while she's sleeping." He exhaled.

Just from his face, I could see that he was serious.

I disregarded his theory and waved him off.

"Look, I got a few things to handle tonight, so you guys can rest easy. If my idea falls out how I planned it, we'll make our move. I really appreciate ya for your loyalty. You a real bad mon." I saluted.

"Save it for when this shit is over, youngin."

After getting my things together, I made my way back outside to the front parking lot and quickly found a private area I could speak in without being heard. Dialing JoJo's number, I waited patiently for him to answer.

"I'm here." His voice came through the line.

"Good. I know this is kinda weird, little bro, but this is our best chance to get in reach of this clown. He's caused too much pain, soldier."

"You know I understand, Rude. I'm just paying attention and taking notes. Dahlia has been back-and-forth to the address, but I have yet to find out how hard it's gonna be to get in," he responded in a low tone.

"Listen just for a minute. Come and meet me at the border of the Westside District, and we can chop it up there. Twenty minutes." I spun in a slow circle to make sure I was at a distance.

"I'm there."

Hanging up my cell, I pondered on what I had JoJo creeping around doing, and it was unfolding at its best. Dahlia had clearly started to jump toward Lo's side right after Seven was murdered. Her purpose to me was useless, but I could see the treachery in her from a mile away. Just like the rest of the snakes, she would be cut down along with the grass, and I knew exactly how to grasp her attention.

Pacing toward my car, I nodded at one of the head Muslim guards for Abdullah before jumping inside. I started my engine and quickly pulled out of the parking lot, keeping my movements to a minimum. At this moment, I couldn't risk his whereabouts. Everything was falling apart, and nearly everyone that had been trusted had proven to be disloyal. My biggest worry was this bitch, Taki. She knew more. She was closer. She was nearly my eyes. That shit had to end.

I was cruising through the west district, viewing all the things we used to be able to enjoy in our city before the storm took it — Club Crucial, the parks, or even Mozley Park.

Peaceful family sections had turned to killers working posts, and in most violent places, children or women didn't want to step out.

A large, black SUV pulled into the intersection and slammed on the brakes in front of me, nearly causing us to collide. My mind went to hit the reverse, but three more sped up from behind and on the side, blocking me in. Within seconds, agents popped their heads from every door, guns aimed directly at my whip.

"You better freeze like it's the fucking Ice Age, son, or I'm gonna empty that skull," one yelled, moving swiftly toward me.

He was followed by three more, and before I knew it, I was being snatched out and thrown to the ground forcefully.

"Well, hello, Mr. Bah. My name is Agent Kent, CIA, and I need to talk to you, motherfucker."

"Fuck you, pussy hole. No cop fear me nun. Remember these streets belong to us, you pig." I looked him in the eyes, ready to spit in his face.

They didn't hesitate to leave my car in the road, throwing me in the back of one of the trucks. They all dispersed in a flash, evacuating the area, knowing that assistance was bound to arrive at any time.

I turned my head, looking at the devil snake that snatched me up.

"You know you're fucking dead, right?"

"You know that shit only applies for the weak ass Atlanta

Police Department. We're the real happy boys, you stupid mud baby, and I'll be glad to prove it." He smiled before a pillowcase was thrown over my head.

I felt the strong butt of a shogun ram into my gut and nearly passed out. I knew these fuck ass agents were definitely going to burn in my backyard. I just had to last forty-eight hours to make it out and ensure it.

DAHLIA

I had been paving my feet to find this guy, Lo, and after a few hard days of work, Lo was already having faith in me to complete his little fantasy mission. I had intentions on running down on him because of Seven's knowledge and past history with this lunatic. He was already a wanted man on my list, but after I saw that Rude Boy was at more of a disadvantage, I found my way to him and placed my bid. Yes, I had every plot to snatch as many zeros as I could from his pockets, but my own plan would have to eventually hit the air, so I could end my journey.

 I had been waiting in Lo's office with him after sliding through on all the other districts about the benefits of gaining Rude Boy's head. Not only would it make my job easier, but it would clear another problem that I had to dodge with him feeling as if I'd sank his ship maliciously. He was truly just a decoy, giving me only so much time. Things were sliding down my side of the field.

Taki bursting through the doors killed my thoughts, and as she strolled past me in her skimpy dress, she was sure to strut a little harder to show off. She was a real arrogant hood bitch that had too much money and power. She was a problem in my story, and her mind was so loose that I could get blown off the cover for her childish manner.

"You arrived here mighty quick to have taken care of so much. Hope everything was covered." She looked back at me before turning her head to Lo.

"The same night you got nearly decapitated at the club was the same night Daffy ends up face first on the floor. Too many open doors that had been closed only by the two of us, also Daffy. Either these peasants have a spy on us, or someone is playing both sides." She looked at him with suspicious eyes

He straightened the collar of his shirt before downing his half full glass of whiskey.

"Fuck you, Taki. I don't know what the hell you're trying to insinuate here, but I'm the reason for all of this shit being in place. We've torn the city to pieces running after a fucking maniac that doesn't want to stop. He wants us dead just as much as we want him. Now, I respect your work and mentality on everything you've applied toward this but never disrespect my loyalty nor my honor."

"Yes, for sure. Who wouldn't want to fuck with me? Still, I'm speaking on something far more valuable here, the steering wheel of this city, because it looks to me that you're probably about to lose it. The Feds are involved, which means we have only so much time before they make this problem another war with the government. If that happens again, I don't think no one will be able to worry about a district or a position ever again."

"Di'meech is handling security in the building for me. I have a bounty on both of their heads so big that the first greedy lowlife will sacrifice their own soul to handle it. I have a plan in effect, but it's not that easy. The superior over the federal bureau owes me favors, and I need those helping hands now. My father is disturbed at his highest, and the wrong move may cost all of us." Lo exhaled, taking a seat.

"No one will hold me accountable for anything that I choose to do. This is a city that's built from a criminal economy. We made the rules after they forced us after a civil catastrophe with the law. I don't recall you having to take a fall in one piece during that time, so our minds are definitely banking on two different objectives. The smartest will always win."

"You're wrong." He gazed up at her from his chair. "Politics will always win."

They were going back-and-forth with one another, and I knew the tragedy of Daffy would surely slow down their momentum on trapping in Rude Boys district to end his reign for good. I needed the most information I could gain on them all. It was bigger than Lo from the sound of things. Either way,

I wasn't stopping until I found out exactly what I needed with this entire group.

"He's only holding on by the hairs attached to his head, and any day now, he could fall if the pressure is raised just a little," I advised, not trying to invade in their dispute.

"And what makes you say that?" Lo asked me.

"Because he's so worried about his girl that he can't focus on his own life to survive a few more days. He knows if he just abandons the situation, you or Taki would most definitely follow him and continue to shed their blood. They're not trying to be on the run. He's trying to end this here, so he can live happily ever after."

Taki approached me slowly, until we were face to face.

"You know more than you say. You've been around him once. You can make it happen again. Find out their location, so we can end this once and for all. Just ensure that my man is in one piece where I can at least have one child before I kill him," she ordered as if she was just the boss.

"Listen, if what you're saying is true, and you can make your way around him and my brother, alert us on the location, and I'll send my men in to do the rest." Lo stood to his feet, overruling her request

"I'll do what I can." I nodded before walking out of the residence.

Neither one of them understood why I was present, neither did they care that I was a walk-in helper that knew more about their mission and problem than they did. That was only because I wasn't there for any of them, including Rude Boy. I needed the leader of the city, and that was Lo's father, the senator of Georgia.

Rude Boy
Location Unknown

AFTER ARRIVING TO WHEREVER THESE ASSHOLES HAD TAKEN me, they forced me to sit down in a chair before snatching the pillowcase from my head. The large lights above my vision nearly blinded me, and it took my eyes a second to adjust to my surroundings. When I was able to see clearly, the face of the pussy, Agent Kent, appeared as if he was God himself.

"Mr. Khalifah Bah, a.k.a. Rude Boy, a.k.a. Asswipe. You know damn well it's not a pleasure, but I can say it is for the CIA. You've been on a radar, Mr. Bah. You've killed, distributed, and enforced pandemonium all over this city. I don't know if you believe in God or not, boy, but I'm damn sure gonna try and force ya." He sat down in the chair directly in front of me.

"Maybe you've bumped your fucking head, or you may just don't care about what you've gotten yourself into. If I'm not released in twenty-four hours, I'll be sure that you will never work with this agency, or in this world, again. You'll be so far buried under the soil that the Lord himself won't waste any time trying to raise you up." I exhaled, trying to keep my temper under control.

"Ain't that what all you little Jamaican people say when they're mad? I can't remember the time when anyone from your little island placed any fear in me or my department. We have rules as well, motherfucker, and that's to not get on our radar unless you really want problems for yourself and the ignorant people standing behind you. Now I know who you are, yeah. I know what you're capable of, but if we believed you were that much of a threat to the CIA, we would have placed a bullet in your head when we stopped you at the light."

"So, why in the fuck am I here now?"

"You're here because I have no one else to take me to the source. You see, we've been investigating this city for years, down to the criminals and terrorists. Even the police department and federal agency. We could have taken anyone and used them as our crash dummies and decoys. You are quite different. You can help us pull this entire thing down, and yes, you and your people get a chance to walk away free from this."

I looked him in the eyes, along with the few agents that were standing in the back. I was more than disgusted with his proposal, and working with his kind was something that I didn't have on my agenda. I needed to ensure that Taki and Lo received their punishment of the grave without second guessing when I left this place. I didn't want a future where I had to look over my shoulder and oppositions taking me out, and I didn't need a stupid motherfucker like this CIA agent forcing something on me that would make shit worse than the situation I was already in.

"I've been in this city for a long time, Kent, and I've ran across slime balls like you the entire time. See, the one thing that you don't understand about this town is the underworld has already sucked it dry. We own these streets. We own the businesses. We own the murderers. Nothing will overrule the rules of Atlantastan, but this is something you already know. That's why you're asking me for my assistance now. I hold a strong hold for my people, and that's another thing that I'm sure you know. If you wanted the source so bad, you could just walk right in and pick him up if it was that easy. You know, just as I do, that if you try that, this city will see the biggest war they have ever seen since the first pandemic. So, my answer is no. You don't have to second guess your mind on me changing it neither because it's not gonna happen."

Agent Kent wore a look of anger on his face. He slammed a hard fist down on the metal table in front of us as if I infuriated him.

"You know what this will cost you, right? We have laws to follow as the security of this state!"

"And we have laws to follow as the criminals and providers of this city."

"Okay, Mr. Bah, we can play it your way. I will win in the end, and you will fall victim to this pathetic city that you crave and love." He walked toward the door with his men leaving out behind him.

~

Agent Jamiyah Porter

Opening my eyes, I realized that it was early in the a.m., and my vision rotated to Ghost standing at the bedroom door that I was occupying.

"Is something wrong?" I asked him as I placed my feet on the floor.

"Oh, it's something more than wrong, but you might wanna get up and grab your gun, so we can try and get the hell away from here and find Rude Boy."

Shuffling to gather the small stuff that I had, I checked my gun before placing it into the holster on my hip.

"What do you mean we have to find Rude Boy?"

He never answered me as we trailed through the hallways that led us to the main living area. When we reached it, I noticed that the nasty woman, Dahlia, was posted next to Abdullah. Seven of his men were standing directly beside them, and they didn't hesitate to raise their guns at us as if we were the new opposition. Ghost immediately stood in front of me as he raised his gun as well.

"I warned you all. Now we have a situation on our hands that needs to be removed from our district immediately. Rude

Boy was snatched by a group of authorities, and your name is written all over this, Agent Porter, if I'm correct." He glared at me with a hateful expression.

"What?! I don't know what you're talking about. Rude Boy left out last night, and I haven't laid eyes on him since. I'm on the same team as him, let alone I have things on my own agenda that I have to settle with Lo as well. Why would I wanna see anything happen to him?"

"Fuck all that. Y'all motherfuckers got guns raised at us, and no one knows for sure what the fuck is going on here, but I would like to know where did this bitch come from out of nowhere, and how in the fuck did she find us?" Ghost pointed a finger at Dahlia.

"I can speak for myself since you aren't man enough to ask me on your own. While you remedial beings have been playing around and dodging the fact that this idiot, Lo, is out for all of your blood, I worked my way into finding out everything we need. The Kiss Squad and Taki is working with whoever possible to bring this shit down to the ground. You may not have more than twenty-four hours to handle this matter, or you, Rude Boy, and every entire district that assisted you will be swept off from the map of this city. Now you can believe me or not, but your opinion for what I'm saying is something I could care less about. Seven is dead, and he was my only reason for even being around you individuals."

"You fucking bitch, you're playing both sides!" I tried to step toward her, but Ghost refrained me from moving.

Abdullah's men were still pointing guns at us, and at that moment, I knew that there were more people working against us that we couldn't see. This Dahlia chick was more than the prime suspect of what I perceived in my mind, and I refused to see her escape without facing her consequences.

"I'll tell all of you like this. Rude Boy is gonna get in contact, and then we'll know and understand exactly who to kill and throw in the fucking ocean. I can say this, Abdullah. She's not the enemy in this situation right now. What I need y'all to do is lower those guns and let's all agree on no one leaving until Rude Boy shows. He'll be able to lead this shit the correct way then. If not, y'all can go ahead and pull the triggers, and most of us can die in this bitch, but I can assure you it won't end how you think." Ghost looked at him with no fear.

He nodded silently with a nasty frown which showed me that I wasn't trusted at all. My cards had fallen wrong so many times dealing with this entire slump, and I could literally say that I wanted to just run off and live the rest of my life dodging the government and anyone else for that matter. All I could think about was putting a bullet through Lo's head for all my suffering, and the more I pondered, I even wanted to kill Taki as well. My spirit had been disheveled ever since my partner, Lace, died, but it was also the reason I wanted to bust my gun until the smoke was clear on this.

Ghost grabbed me by the arm and stepped a short distance away, so no one could hear his words but me.

"I don't know what the fuck is going on, but if you got any flaky shit stirred up to save your own ass, it won't work."

"What the hell are you talking about? I've stood right here this entire time through this whole ordeal because I want this motherfucker just as bad as Rude Boy do. Save myself from what? I'm the one who killed the fucking agent. I only held firm this long just so he could gain his little girlfriend back and execute the idiot that took her."

"You smell like a bitch in love with a street thug. You need to be all the way open with this shit. You can get everybody killed moving off some first sight criminal love shit. Now is the time to be useful with every resource you got to fast forward this shit like now."

"I clearly understand everything you're saying without you yanking on me, nigga. I've been doing just that, and I'm the one who's telling him to flush this dumbass and kill him. I found the address to his main penthouse suite at the bottom of midtown. District 1."

"Yeah, it don't faze me. I'm made for this shit. Try convincing that to him, so this shit can proceed. I got my own shit to take care of. Guess we'll know when he shows." He walked away.

I knew shit was risky trying to outrun the same people I'd just worked side by side with, some of the smartest. I was just a good worker, and once I exterminated this problem, I was pushing on to let the same motherfuckers eat my trails as I stepped elsewhere.

TAKI

I had just gotten up late at night to prepare myself for the day that was ahead. I was rearranging a few things from Lo's current rule list, and I had the approval of one of the highest. It turned out that I wasn't the only one that felt like his leadership was borderline poor. After the poor senator of state happened to reach out, I soaked in the understanding of what my new plan was to receive my sweet ass victory. As they said sometimes, it was not about what you knew. It was about who you knew.

Watching my cellular ring, I answered it through my Bluetooth.

"Kiss speaking." I hummed through the line.

"Pleasure. I know that we have no need for speaking on why this call is being placed, but a meeting will be needed in due time. I'm assisting however need be. Just get my baby son back, and whatever you want is yours. As far as my son, Lo, consider him excused."

"That sounds interesting." I stood to my feet. "But that's not it. Ruling over Atlantastan has been written in law that every dictator has to stand firmly on all actions, and injustice betrayal within this town has been at its highest since Lo has been in the chair. Since you left, he has made nothing but a disaster. I will give it two years, and the authorities and state will have this state back in control. You pay us to keep it out. If I'm working for you, I get the position. I hold the authority, and I sign the contracts to all that refutes what we are implementing. I want Kiss Squad to have the entire Atlantastan. Then, I make your money." I bargained through the line.

He was quiet for a second before speaking, but I knew that my offer was one to die for, or he would die, and that was so simple.

"I've made my objectives pretty clear, and as to your question, yes. My son has tarnished this city's reputation, along with my economy status for the last few years. I'm never the one to cross out family, but as of right now, this is about business. Complete the task and Atlantastan is yours." He agreed.

"May your sweet soul rest easy tonight, Senator. All your worries belong to me now." I smiled before ending the call.

Messaging a few different members of my crew, I ordered them to gather up our best shooters from each side. We needed this strike, and the Lord knew I was about to receive it in full.

Just the look of Rude Boy begging for his life... I could taste it.

∼

Rude Boy

THE MORNING WAS SURFACING FAST, AND I COULD FEEL THE breeze of the sharp wind cutting across my face. Those dirty ass agents had more than a hidden agenda, and I was going to be aware, so I could drain their souls one by one. The authorities were square face enemies with any street member and organizations since the last big sweep of so many legends before this city turned to hell. All I could think about was murdering all these idiots, even if it killed me.

Hearing the sound of a car pulling slowly in behind me, I paused and turned around to JoJo behind the tinted Dodge Charger.

I wasted no time jumping into the passenger seat, and he immediately hit the gas, speeding out of the secluded parking lot.

"How in the fuck did you know where I was?" I asked, stalking the rearview mirror to ensure we weren't being followed.

"I followed after they snatched you at the light. I was coming down the street when they were speeding away. I didn't want to ignite any gunfire with those people until I confirmed you were good," he replied as he focused on the road.

"You're my guardian angel soldier. Big respect for the action. Now that we found out exactly what we need, it's time to mash the gas on this shit. Stop by Abdullah's to grab the rest of our team. It's on you now, shotta. We clearing the scene until we get in there." I exhaled anxiously.

"I'm ready," was all he said before we crossed back over into the Westside District.

~

Agent Jamiyah Porter

It had been the same thing for the past several hours, nothing but tension between us and the district leaders' minions. I was growing impatient with the insults, and everything in my body wanted me to just snap into battle mode and really show my capabilities. Instead, I paced back-and-forth out on the back patio until JoJo and Rude Boy walked through the front door of Abdullah's estate.

"Where the fuck did you disappear to? These assholes came up with the conspiracy that I had you snatched by the law, let alone walking down on us as if they were ready to murder me on the spot." I fumed when I crossed the room to look him in the face.

"What? That's impossible because I didn't alert no one to what I was heading to do."

"Well, the air needs to be cleared, Rude Boy. This is an agent of the law. Maybe even one that snatched the lives of our elite when all this began. Trust is hard for that on all platforms, so yes, we didn't hesitate to look in her direction. If she didn't play a part in it, who did? We have a murder on sight policy with police, and they ambushed you on the borders of my space. That's never happened in this district since I've been the backbone. Is there more to this story that I'm not understanding?" Abdullah asked humbly with his bundle of gunmen behind him.

"First of all, I explained about her when we arrived, so my word is firm from the first statement, boss man. You don't have any right to question me more. Yes, this is deeper than I expected, and the CIA is the one cooking up some sneaky shit. This bloodshed is because of me accepting filthy intention motherfuckers in my safe zone. I'll go against everyone that threatens that, even if that means my district go head up with the law again. I'll die on that. We only got a few hours to take the first shot, and I'm raging until I scratch all their names from my memory. We need to go like now."

I shook my head at Abdullah before grabbing my bag that was sitting in the corner.

"And what about this bitch? She just reappears from thin air with all the advice. Are you sure she's standing even footed on this side because we're risking it all when we move after this." I cut my eyes over to Dahlia.

"Dahlia, where have you been? You go missing for days in the mix of business and reappear. That would have a lot of us scratching our heads." Rude Boy questioned.

"Damn sho got me scratching mines," Ghost added in as he posted against the wall.

"Expecting me to move like you guys is something that will never happen. I came to take care of business, not die while trying to handle it. If I see that we have stragglers, I will separate until this shit begins to steer correctly."

I ate up the little lie, knowing that shit was difficult when you played in this type of field. You had to be prepared for anything to fall, especially the ones that were beside you.

I shook my head, knowing that I had to bury my hatchet and make sure it counted.

"It's time to head out. I'm spacing out and picking backup for us just in case. If we gotta take that whole building down tomorrow just to get to this fuckboy, we will. We move together. We come out together." Rude Boy said, trying to give us all the fuel we could use. I was prepared to give up whatever I needed to watch all of them bleed. Now I was going to show it.

AGENT JAMIYAH PORTER

District 1
17th Street Lofts

My adrenaline was beating like a bass drum, and we were literally about to make a statement with the choice Rude Boy was making. I never wanted to see a criminal die so bad, so much to the point where it slowly turned me into one. We were parked across the street at the gas station, waiting for our signal. I happened to be crammed in the car with this sneaky bitch, Dahlia, and each time my eyes met with hers, I felt a cold, black-hearted enemy. I even forced Rude Boy to make everyone ditch their phones before we proceeded, so no one could potentially sidetrack us from what was at stake.

When the signal was made, I watched JoJo exit the car in front of us, and he proceeded into the building. Rude Boy immediately gave us the nod, and we were all out of the car, making our way inside. I spotted a Kiss Squad member approaching us from the left side of my peripheral. His kiss-stained shirt gave him away. We didn't need the action breaking off in the streets with so many civilians at risk, not to mention the crooked FBI and CIA that would easily get involved.

It was exactly how I envisioned because the man reached to pull his gun. Ghost wasted no time firing off three shots into his chest.

Boc! Boc! Boc!

The screams erupted immediately, and people started to scatter.

"We might wanna speed this up!" Ghost yelled as he entered the building first. Me, Dahlia, and Rude Boy followed, and once we reached the lobby, two more men appeared with guns aimed straight for us. The gunfire started to release, and at that moment, I knew that there was no turning around.

JoJo

After sliding into my brother's residence unnoticed, I quickly made my way to the double set of elevators. I didn't even get a chance to get the doors closed before the sound of bullets started to erupt in my ear. Our timeframe was critical at this point, and I never thought that I would see the day where I would be standing on the opposite side of my big brother, but today was that day.

As the elevator doors came open, I stepped out and witnessed Di'meech posted at the end of the hallway as if he had been expecting me. I knew that he'd spotted me the last time I showed up to watch my brother's movements so that we could proceed with our mission.

"You were prepared to die today. It's so sad how family could betray you, but Lo asked me to divide you real nice, so we won't have any problem flushing you."

He removed his pistol and started to fire recklessly at me.

Boom! Boom! Boom! Boom!

I ran for cover, leaping behind the side wall next to me. I knew that this guy was dangerous with a gun, but I just needed to get my hands on him. I quickly opened and slammed the exit door behind me and pulled my black hunting knife from the hip.

I waited patiently, feeling my heart speed up from being so still. Once I spotted an inch of his gun, I slapped his hand with all my might and tried to jam my blade in him with the other.

"Shitttt!" he yelled when it gouged a chunk out of his arm.

I landed a two piece to his face, and he stood back quickly, ramming a vicious uppercut in my side.

I stumbled, rolling against the wall, before we stood off again. I didn't have time to wrestle with this guy, and I knew if I made the wrong move, he would kill me for sure.

He rushed me and began to swing. I dodged the first three, and he landed a stiff one on my right ear. Before he could sing again, I used my left hand to jam the knife straight up into his esophagus.

His movements froze, and the blood that splattered across my clothes assured me that this fight was over. I could feel his dead weight rising, and I quickly pushed him to the side, watching his lifeless body crumble to the floor.

I pulled my gun and took a few seconds to catch my breath. Pushing forward to the front door of my brother's loft, I opened the door and rushed in.

The cool breeze of cigar smoke lingered in the air, and the massive space looked like a luxurious museum. There were paintings, antiques, expensive wine, and everything else a person could ask for. I looked past all the valuables, creeping slowly through his home.

Spotting the open balcony door, I walked through it, feeling the sun graze my skin. The sound of two gunshots firing off grabbed my attention. I could feel the sharp thrust that penetrated my side, forcing me to drop to the ground.

"My brother, my own brother!" I watched as Lo crept from around the large air conditioning unit.

He walked down on me as I gritted my teeth to fight the pain of his bullet. His right foot kicked my gun farther away from me.

"You're not my brother, just like your father isn't my father. I would never represent what you all stand for as a bloodline, and that's why you won't win, dick head." I laughed at him, knowing he wouldn't hesitate to kill me.

I prayed that Rude Boy executed him and moved forward with his plan. I knew that his rage would only grow more out of control if bit.

"Lo, drop the fucking gun before I empty, you son of a bitch." I heard Agent Porter's voice.

Agent Jamiyah Porter

WE ENDED UP CREATING THE BIGGEST SHOOTOUT AS WE MADE our way toward the top of this building. Besides a graze on my arm, we were perfectly fine. My head was so persistent on getting my hands on this bastard that I didn't even recognize the damage we were causing. Ghost ended up splitting up on the tenth floor after we ran into a few of Taki's soldiers. Me, Rude Boy, and Dahlia didn't hesitate to take the exit stairs all the way up to the seventeenth floor.

I aimed my gun before I stepped through the door and then

paused at the sight of the assassin's dead body sprawled out on the floor.

"JoJo," Rude Boy whispered. "Keep going."

We stepped in unison all the way to Lo's loft and noticed the large front door was open. I flushed in with my gun raised. My attention led me to the patio door, and that was when I spotted Lo hovering over JoJo with his gun aimed.

"Lo, drop the gun before I empty, you son of a bitch!"

His eyes rotated up to me with anger, and I didn't flinch a muscle with my aim.

"You idiots really have crossed the ultimate boundary. You came into my home; you've betrayed my family with lies to have them fighting against me. You jeopardized my seat at this table with no respect for my position. So, how do you think this will end?"

"It's only gonna end with you dying, pussy boy. Along with Taki."

"CIA! All of you put your fucking hands up! Rude Boy, drop it!" Dahlia snapped.

I couldn't believe my fucking ears, but something in me said that I wasn't stupid by a long shot. This bitch was too weird, exactly what I warned Rude Boy against — the law having a direct target on us, someone that would be right under our noses.

"You snake ass bitch! I knew I could smell you. I seen it in your movements." I still kept my gun aimed on Lo as I cut my eyes at her.

"Tough luck, Agent Porter. This isn't the time or place to explain this misunderstanding, but I can't allow this to happen. Rude Boy, drop the gun. Now!" she warned with her gun pointed toward his head.

He did as she asked, but my sight caught Ghost appearing behind her as if he was summoned like a demon.

"Did you think you were the only one watching, bitch? I didn't need goggles to peep you either. Now you drop your fucking gun."

"Fuck this," Lo shouted before raising his gun.

I fired one slug, catching him in the chest.

Boom!

His gun dropped as he stumbled toward me in a sluggish manner. I delivered a foot kick to his chin, forcing him to fly backwards until he tumbled right over the roof top.

"Arghhhhhhh!"

His screams echoed until he reached the ground floor, landing on God knows what.

I immediately turned my gun on Dahlia, staring down in her eyes as I approached her.

"I'm a CIA agent of this law, and you don't override the law, Agent Porter. Lower your gun, Agent." She gave me an order, sounding like my crooked superior.

"Your position doesn't matter in this law, and you don't override the code on this side, bitch. I don't have a superior." I dismissed her statement and fired a bullet straight in between the center of her eyes.

Boom!

Her head snapped back, causing Ghost to jump out of the way, before her body crashed to the ground.

"You could've winked your eye or something. Crazy ass bitch." Ghost exhaled before walking off.

I helped JoJo to his feet before Rude Boy came over to assist me. He looked me in the eyes with deep sincerity.

"Thank you. I know your journey with this is at an end. I still have another problem to deal with," he said before tossing JoJo's arm around his shoulder.

"Well, I guess I still have a problem as well. I'm a wanted fugitive now, and I guess a cop killer as well. We might wanna make our way outta here before this shit is barricaded in," I responded as we rushed to exit the premises.

We took the elevator and arrived downstairs. I could hear the police sirens at a far distance, and I knew we only had a certain amount of time before shit got ugly with the law.

Upon us exiting the building, the sound of gunshots sounding off forced me to snap in action.

Boc! Boc! Boc! Boc! Boc! Boc! Boc!

I ducked low just as Rude Boy was struck in his stomach with a bullet, crumbling to the ground with JoJo.

"Fuckk!" He winced in pain before clutching on to his wound.

My eyes locked in on the crazy bitch, Taki, aiming to kill with a look of fire in her eyes. I locked in my aim and released every shot that I could until she disappeared into the alleyway across the street.

Bending down, I grabbed Rude Boy's wound, trying to stop the blood from rushing. I noticed Ghost swerve up to the sidewalk with the car and jump out to assist me.

He grabbed Rude Boy, tossing him over his shoulder before I dragged JoJo under the arms to the car. By the time we were pulling off into the opposite direction, you could view the SWAT team and undercover SUVs that were swerving up to the center.

"Shit! Shit! Shit!" I panicked, trying to stop the blood Rude Boy was losing. He was going in and out of consciousness, and this was the last thing I needed, trying to fight a two-sided battle.

"Hey, stay awake. Do you hear me?" I tapped the side of his face repeatedly, trying to force him out the slump.

"Just keep him awake. I know where we can take him!" Ghost yelled as he bent a left turn.

"How about the fucking hospital? He's dying!"

"We can't. The police will be all over that shit. Just hold on." He ignored my request.

I watched Rude Boy's eyes slowly begin to roll, and I quickly started to perform CPR.

"Oh, no, you fucking don't. You're gonna help me finish this. You can't die, motherfucker." I pressed down on his chest with force.

For some strange reason, I felt like crying about this man.

He had slowly become a part of my journey while trying to fight my way out of the ditch I placed myself into. I knew two things for sure. I officially chose what side I wanted to be on, and Taki would die along with everyone else for the chaos she placed upon us.

"Ghost, hurry the fuck up. He's not breathing." I continued to perform CPR, praying he held on...

To Be Continued
ATLANTASTAN 3
Bleed in Harmony

REVIEW

Did you enjoy the read?
Let us know how much by leaving us a review on Amazon and Goodreads.

OTHER BOOKS BY

URBAN AINT DEAD

Tales 4rm Da Dale

The Hottest Summer Ever

Hittin' Licks For The Holidays: Atlanta

Wet Dreams On Lockdown: The Nurse

How To Publish A Book From Prison

By **Elijah R. Freeman**

Despite The Odds

By **Juhnell Morgan**

Good Girls Gone Rogue

Good Girls Gone Rouge 2

By **Manny Black**

Hittaz

Hittaz 2

Hittaz 3

Hittaz 4

Coldhearted

By **Lou Garden Price, Sr.**

Charge It To The Game

Charge It To The Game 2

A Summer To Remember With My Hitta

Snatched Up By A Hitta

Santa Sent Me A Real One For Christmas

Wet Dreams on Lockdown: The Unit Manager

Thug Me The Right Way 2

Thug Me The Right Way 3

Seizing A Gangsta's Heart For The Summer

By **Nai**

A Setup For Revenge

Wet Dreams On Lockdown: The Librarian

By **Ashley Williams**

Ridin' For You

Ridin' For You, Too

Trickin' on a Heaux for Christmas: A BBW Love Story

Homie Hoppin' For The Holidays

Wet Dreams on Lockdown: The Female C.O

Letters Of His Love

By **Telia Teanna**

The State's Witness

The State's Witness 2

The State's Witness 3

This Time Won't You Save Me

This Time Won't You Save Me 2

His Summer Side Piece

By **Kyiris Ashley**

Stuck In The Trenches

Stuck In The Trenches 2

By **Huff Tha Great**

The Swipe

The Swipe 2

By **Toōla**

Melted the Heart of a Menace

Wet Dreams On Lockdown: Lieutenant Grace

By P. Wise

Merry Trapmas: Ice & Frost

By **Mia Sky**

Thug Me The Right Way

By **DiamondATL & Nai**

Atlantastan

By **Chris Green**

IN The Streetz

By **Tron Hill**

Wet Dreams on Lockdown: The Male C.O

By **Tamyra Griffin**

Wet Dreams On Lockdown: The Counselor

By **Paris Iman**

Wet Dreams On Lockdown: The Warden

By **Shawnice**

Wet Dreams On Lockdown: The Captain

By **TN Jones**

COMING SOON FROM

Urban Aint Dead

The Hottest Summer Ever 2

THE G-CODE

Tales 4rm Da Dale 2

How To Invest In The Stock Market From Prison

By **Elijah R. Freeman**

Hittaz 5

Coldhearted 3

By **Lou Garden Price, Sr.**

The Swipe 3

By **Toola**

Good Girls Gone Rogue 3

By **Manny Black**

COMING SOON FROM

Despite The Odds 2
Hittin' Licks For The Holidays: Chicago
By **Juhnell Morgan**

Charge It To The Game 3
By **Nai**

A Setup For Revenge 2
By **Ashley Williams**

This Time Won't You Save Me 3
By **Kyiris Ashley**

Ridin' Forever
By **Telia Teanna**

Atlantastan 3
By **Chris Green**

IN The Streetz 2
By **Tron Hill**

BOOKS BY

URBAN AINT DEAD's C.E.O

Elijah R. Freeman

Triggadale

Triggadale 2

Triggadale 3

Tales 4rm Da Dale

The Hottest Summer Ever

Murda Was The Case

Murda Was The Case 2

Murda Was The Case 3

Hittin' Licks For The Holidays: Atlanta

Wet Dreams On Lockdown: The Nurse

How To Publish A Book From Prison

STAY CONNECTED

Follow
Elijah R. Freeman
On Social Media
FB: Elijah R. Freeman
IG: @the_future_of_urban_fiction

Printed in the USA
CPSIA information can be obtained
at www.ICGtesting.com
CBHW050343091024
15608CB00009B/473

9 798990 470187